BY DION LACK

Cover Illustration by Olie Boldador
Illustrations by Stan Ford

LackToast
ENTERTAINMENT

Library of Congress Cataloging-in-Publication Data

Lack, Dion.
Voyage of Truth/ by Dion Lack.
Edited by Twilla A. Tanyi

ISBN- 13: 978-0-9970333-0-4
ISBN- 10: 0-9970333-0-4

Praises to the almighty God
Thanks to my amazing girls Kaylee, Brookie, Dawnise and Twillz

Voyage of Truth is based off of stories
inspired by my late mother.

INTRODUCTION

Voyage of Truth takes place 1.5 million kilometers from the sun on the aquatic planet Kepler. It's sectioned into 12 divisions, all governed by their own treaties. Inside each division are thousands of enormous residential ships, known as city ships, bartering their resources. Each boat carries tens of thousands of phages, the resident species of Kepler.

In each of the 12 divisions, there are mother ships called Beverods; engineered by an elite group of legislators: the Iotas. Each Beverod enforces their own set of laws with strict supervision on their city ships. Kepler is a socioeconomic planet in which all the divisions follow the Extermination & Bartering Process (EBP). Every ship has developed one high demanding resource to exchange for another ship's resource. This communist order of interdependency is how the planet survives.

All the city ships have developed their own languages, and residents share identical birthmarks across their arms and chest. This birthmark is the intravenous design of their exposed circulatory system. Phages are born with three-fingers on each hand, two-toes on each foot. All city ships have an admiral, captain and an authoritative, civil force called maphletes. All ships are named after their omnipresent admiral.

Phages are born to exterminate intruders like Variables or Leviathans from their home ships. By doing so, they receive payment in quota points (QP). By reaching the given quota, they are protected from being selected for the purging ceremony.

Variables are parasitic creatures that feed on the ship's internal structure. They reside in the 12 divided oceans and frequently pirate ships whenever they stop to barter. Variables are harmless, but they can become belligerent when threatened.

Phages are equipped with an extermination weapon called an Arm Cannon (AC). It's an ever-evolving glove that fires from the palm to weaken or destroy intruders. Each AC has a reloadable ammunition chamber and strength dial to adjust its force.

PART I

CHAPTER 1

Slumped over in a metal chair, a beaten soldier awakens disoriented and confused. He jumps up hitting his head on a lampshade just as his handcuffs yanks him back into his seat. The cold metal slicing into his skin causes him to realize that his Arm Cannon (AC) has been confiscated. The dangling light helps him make out images in this dark, secluded room. He uses his shoulder to wipe sweat from his cheek and a sharp pain vibrates through his jaw. He instantly remembers his brief struggle before he was knocked out. The man tries his strength to lift the chair off it its legs but fails. It's somehow magnetized to the ground along with a matching table infront of him. On top he spots a manila folder with names on it. *Officer Grae*. He stretches forward and drags the folder closer with his chin. He bites the top flap and opens the file to read. It reveals his personal data in detail and all the crimes he has commited.

"What in the world?" Grae uses his chin to swipe to the second page and finds dozens of candid pictures and documented conversations with friends. Defeated, Grae slams his head on the table. "Yup, this is it. There's no talking your way out of this one. You should've gotten out when you had the chance."

Suddenly a revolving door reels open and the room's florescent light powers on. Grae pops up predicting the worse. He watches a woman whistling enter inside and lock the door with a keypad.

1

"Welcome officer." She struts forward with exotic weapons bouncing off her hips and sits on the edge of the table. She crosses her legs and smiles, "I'm so glad to finally meet you Grae. Can I get you anything? Water or juice?"

"How about the key to these handcuffs."

She laughs. "In due time. I just want to ask you a few questions first."

Grae cries. "Where am I?"

"There is nothing for you to worry about. You're on the safest level on this ship which is our Iota interrogation loft."

"Iota? Whoa, I think you all taking my misdenmenors a little too serious now?"

"No sin is smaller than the next."

"I disagree."

"And that's the problem. We're living in a world that loves to compare our struggles and justifies them according to acceptance. But the truth is the Arvelee wants you purged off this ship no matter what."

"For what?"

"Let's skip past that because we have the power to expunge everything you've commited. We - I can see that you have good intentions and can be used immensely in our organization."

"With all due respect, I wouldn't be caught dead working for the Iotas. You are all crooked."

She ignores the insult and uses a finger to comb her red hair over her ear. She adjusts her glasses and picks up his folder. "Theft, vandalism, card possession, disorderly conduct, public intoxication, assault and 4 counts of trespassing. Grae I don't think you have much of a choice. I'm willing to make all this go away."

Grae shrugs. "In exchange for what?"

The mysterious woman smiles and seductively asks, "To help us find Nulo?"

Grae frowns. "What makes you think I know where he's at?"

She grabs a hand full of pictures and deals them on his lap. "Because we've seen the two of you together and we know you're secretly planning something. All you have to do is find Nulo, wearing this tracking device and let us hear what he knows."

Grae leans back in the chair and sighs. "How did I get myself into this?"

TWO DAYS EARLIER

Grae hides in a dark of control booth towering over an empty arena. He checks the time and sighs, "Where is this fool?" Grae uses the booth's computer to begin a search. He type in his username and selects a beacon tracker option. As he hits enter, Grae hears footsteps climbing the ladder below. He ducks his head and tucks himself alongside the wall.

The latch from the door rattles and Grae prepares his arm cannon to fire. He waits for the hooded figure to completely enter the control room and points his AC against its head. Grae slams the door, "It's about time you showed up. Sultri?" He snatches the hood off. "Who are you? What are you doing here?"

"What do you mean, what I'm doing here?" retorts the confused officer. "I'm scheduled to work. What are *you* doing here?"

Embarrassed, Grae sticks his chest out and yells, "Hey, I'm the one asking the questions here! I have a gun, okay? What's your name?"

"Rhoddy, Officer Rhoddy."

"Okay, *Rhoddy*, here's the deal. I'm not gonna hurt you as long as you cooperate. I'm looking for a buddy of mine named Sultri."

As Grae is speaking, he sees Rhoddy's fingers reaching for a button. Grae quickly crushes them with a slamming, fist.

"Argh!" Rhoddy yells. "You just said you weren't here to hurt me."

"What does that button do?"

"It's the anchor. I was trying to prepare the Arvelee for the next barter. My shift started twenty minutes ago and the other city ship will be here any minute now. So if you don't mind, I need to get back to work."

To Rhoddy's surprise, Grae answers, "Go ahead."

"That's it? No gut punching or slapping me around telling me how disrespectful I am?"

"No." Grae laughs. "What type of friends do you have? I'm just gonna hang back here, let you do what you got to do and wait until Sultri arrives."

"Well, you're wasting your time because I never heard of a *Sultri*. This has always been my shift and if he told you he'd be working it, he lied."

"Alright." Grae drops the tough guy attitude. "I'm sorry about this. I think I've been duped again by my *former* friend and another customer. So, we good now?"

Rhoddy holds his throbbing wrist and nods. "Yeah."

Grae reaches for his backpack of memory cards and prepares to leave.

With his back turned, Rhoddy fearfully presses the previous button and screams, "Help, someone's trying to hijack the Arvelee! He's armed and dangerous."

Grae quickly tasers Rhoddy before he can finish his sentence. "Really?" Grae yanks him to the ground in total shock.

4

Suddenly a voice from the intercom responds, "Go ahead, Officer, could you repeat that?"

"Answer him," Grae demands. "Tell them everything is under control."

"I'm sorry, false alarm. I fixed the problem."

Grae forcibly lifts Rhoddy up and says, "What was *that* for? I just asked you whether we were good, and you said yes."

Trying to catch his breath, Rhoddy says, "I'm just trying to protect the ship."

"And you really think I'm trying to hijack our home? I told you I was *only* here looking for Sultri because he owes me quota points. That's all."

Rhoddy gathers himself. "Okay, okay, I panicked. Let's figure this out together and I'll help you find him."

Grae scoffs. "What makes you think I should start believing you now? You're hiding something from me, aren't you?"

"No. I don't even know what this guy looks like."

"We'll see." Grae removes Rhoddy's arm cannon and tightly tapes his wrists and ankles together.

Grae attempts to stick tape over Rhoddy's mouth and he squirms away, saying, "Wait, listen. I wasn't lying about the bartering part. I really am the officer scheduled for the booth now. If I don't start prep soon, maphletes will be notified and we'll *both* be arrested. Please untie me, sir; this job can be very stressful when you're running late."

Grae shrugs. "I'm sorry, but I still can't trust anything you say. For the sake of the Arvelee, you're gonna walk me through everything that needs to be done."

Without much of a choice, Rhoddy surrenders. "Alright."

Grae follows his detailed instructions and flips a combination of switches inside the booth.

The two massive city ships slowly approach each other with port bumpers extended. The ships gently collide, sending a deep trembling vibration throughout the lower levels.

Grae looks past the storm and into the opposite tower window of the attached city ship. He notices a female barter officer inside the illuminated booth and salutes her with a courteous wave. "Hey, you're cute. I see you over there looking at me." The Delione barter officer gives an innocent wave in return and he starts an imaginary conversation with her. "Oh, so you *do* think I'm handsome, huh? Then why are you in that booth way over there and not in this one with me?" Grae flicks his eyebrows and blows a kiss at her.

Rhoddy sighs. "Will you stop flirting and finish the routine? Pull that lever on the right before the boats drift apart."

Grae does it, and asks, "Now what?"

"Now you have to be an official officer and debrief the escorts."

Grae sighs. Before leaving, Grae gags Rhoddy with more tape and wraps his torso around a pole. He says, "Now don't do anything stupid while I'm gone." He hops out of the tower control booth and walks near the crew of eager barter escorts standing in line. Grae clears his throat and shifts back to his tough guy character. "For the new faces I don't recognize; I'm going to give you a quick recap of your job. Drop off our MEG cases and follow the person in front of you. Simple. You are escorts. You are not fighters; that's what the lieutenants are for. So if anything out of the ordinary happens over on the Delione, be smart and get right back here."

The barter escorts nod and grab a temporary boarding card to enter the foreign city ship. They insert the cards into their tactile digital assistant (TDA) gloves and prepare to cross. Each of the escorts are handed the Arvelee's bartering resource, MEG capsules, which stands for Mobile Electronic Generators.

"Remember what I said." Grae encourages the escorts. "And make me look good."

Grae enters his booth. "Did you see that, Rhoddy? Did you see how I handled them?"

Still gagged, Rhoddy mumbled, "How?"

Grae is reminded and snatches the tape off his lips. "Sorry about that. What do I need to do next?"

"Hold down the intercom and report yourself to a maphlete."

Grae smiles. "Good one. You almost got me."

. . . .

Hundreds of lieutenants enter the arena; stretching their muscles and prepping their arm cannon gloves with formulated ammunition; better known as formunition.

The aristocratic Iota members enter the balcony of the mezzanine to be entertained during the upcoming barter. Only elite maphletes are welcome inside the exclusive balcony with the Iotas. The bistro towers high above the arena and is fully protected by ballistic glass.

Before the fighting starts, the Iotas place bets on their favorite lieutenant and predict their upcoming Variable kills.

Several groups of lieutenants join in cheering and barking at one another to motivate themselves for the upcoming Extermination & Bartering Process also known as EBP. The cynical Lieutenant Kaphir is one of the few who is not aroused by the routine battle that lies ahead. He holds his cigar with his teeth and pats his clothing, searching for his lighter. A nearby officer nudges Kaphir with a lit match. "Here, sir."

Kaphir leans his cigar bud into the fire and asks, "How long is the barter scheduled?"

The young officer stutters, "I'm sorry but I don't know. This is my very first EBP and I'm just excited to help out any way I can." He hands Lieutenant Kaphir a clip of formunition, standing awkwardly next him. Kaphir tightens his eye patch behind his head and reminds himself in a whisper, "Just two more days of this nonsense and I am done with this foolery." Kaphir looks up at the applauding elites in the balcony and grins. "Yep. I'll be up there soon, sipping on a tall glass of elixir, laughing at you all playing gladiator." The confused young officer continues to load Kaphir's AC, dramatically signaling him towards the planks.

From a distance, a lone, hideous looking Variable climbs inside the arena. A number of lieutenants laugh at his audacity. "Ah, look at that guy."

"Hey fella, you're all by yourself?"

"Yeah, he's a brave one."

"Aww, are you going to take on all of us?"

Suddenly, the elite erupt with anticipation from the sight of Variables finally entering the mezzanine. "Here come the rest."

The Variables rise out of the freezing ocean and climb the walls of the stalled ships, invading the seemingly unsecured docks. Innumerous moaning Variables pour inside the mezzanine and ransack the arena, searching for nourishment. The lieutenants encourage the crowd of Iota members to cheer louder.

. . . .

ZROOM, ZROOM, ZROOM! The fleet of lieutenants fire rapidly at the roaming hissing Variables. Higher profile lieutenants strategize to perform difficult shots to impress their Iota sponsors in the balcony.

The most celebrated lieutenant of the Arvelee is a veteran: Lieutenant Nulo. He is the crowd favorite, but his pompous actions always keep him in a whirlwind of trouble.

Nulo bounces between casual conversation and assisting other phages with extraordinary strikes and fatalities. He carefully chooses his battles with the sole intention to wow his audience by demonstrating unimaginable moves.

He singles out a larger-than-average Variable sneaking along the south wall. He aims his AC at a pillar. The shot skims past the heads of his fellow shipmates, bounces off the steel pillar and smacks the Variable in the hip, causing it to disintegrate.

Nulo rolls onto his back and points his rifle at a Variable crawling along the ceiling. He looks through his scope and fires at the surface around the Variable, knocking it loose. The Variable flaps its limbs, dropping directly on top of him. Nulo fires and splatters the Variable's ashes onto surrounding lieutenants. "Hey, watch it," a repugnant soldier yells.

Nulo sarcastically chuckles and says, "Sorry about that. Oh, remind me to do the laundry of everyone who's afraid to get a little dirty." Nulo puffs out his chest, dancing through the evil looks and continues to entertain the balcony guests.

. . . .

A clumsy lieutenant franticly sprints towards the mezzanine. He descends a set of stairs two at a time, and enters the long corridor on the mezzanine while sliding an arm cannon glove onto his three fingered palm. "Cretchit." He checks his TDA and accelerates faster through the active pedestrians. "Excuse me, coming through. Move out of the way."

He reaches the mezzanine entrance, scans his TDA and the computerized voice chimes, "Welcome, Lieutenant Sultri. You will be fined 100 quota points for your tardiness."

Lieutenant Sultri drops his head and slaps the wall. "Cretchit, Cretchit."

The arena door opens and Sultri joins the crawling Variable extermination with the other lieutenants.

Their four adhesive paws allow the Variables to scale walls of any kind. A set of sizzling Variables drop drastically from the ceiling and Sultri sighs once he realizes they're Nulo's kills.

Nulo passively pushes Sultri out of his spotlight and blows kisses towards the Iota as they stand in ovation. He takes a quick bow and returns a wink at an attractive Iota female observer behind the glass. "Hope to see you later."

Nulo climbs on top a pile of rubble and yells, "Listen up my fellow lieutenants. I got an exclusive new move I'm about to release. This is a surefire way to gain exposure from the sponsors up there watching, so you're more than welcome to steal it. It's called 'The Snipe Knife'. Don't blink because you just might miss it."

10

Nulo quickly looks over his shoulder and performs a standing back flip. While upside down he fires at a Variable between his legs. A galloping Variable gets smacked in the chin across the arena and is dead before it hits the ground. Once again, Iotas roar in response to his latest move.

Nulo's best friend, Lieutenant Opha, finally hooks up with him. "I think you enjoy this way too much."

Nulo acts dumbfounded. "Whaaaaat?"

"Come on now. The crowd—everyone, cheering for help."

Nulo laughs. "Hey, I'm just doing my job."

"Yeah, okay. Whoa, watch out behind you." Opha quickly shoots a stampeding Variable over the shoulder of his friend.

Nulo cringes from the close blast. "What was that, O? Are you crazy?" He taps his neck to feel for damage from Opha's shot.

Opha utters, "That was me doing my part."

"Leave all the shooting to me."

Opha chuckles at Nulo's discreet insult and watches him backpedal into action. Opha follows and says, "A simple 'thanks' would've been just fine."

"For what?"

"I just saved your life from that Variable?"

Nulo mocks him. "Saved my life from a Variable? Ha. This is just a cheap way to keep us in shape and the elite entertained. If I ever get as much of a scratch from a Variable, I want you to do the honor of putting an AC to my head."

"You're missing the point."

"There's no point to be made, O. If you can't support me out here trying to better myself, you're just as bad as my adversaries. And you know there are a lot of them."

"Listen, I'm trying my best to cut your enemies in half and make you likeable."

"I'll always have enemies. If everyone likes me, it means I'm doing something wrong. And you can thank me later for those words of wisdom."

"Thank you for what? I'm not the one with enemy problems." Nulo evades the arms of a galloping Variable and shoots it in the chest without responding. Opha backs into Nulo and whispers, "When will arrogant Nulo grow up? Everyone knows you are good. Be humble with it."

"Huh? I didn't hear you. I was busy protecting the ship from these dangerous Variables as you claim. You should join me sometime."

"See? You are doing it again."

"Doing what?"

"Childishly looking for attention. I know the real Nulo outside these walls."

Nulo finally stops firing and yells, "What do you want from me?"

Opha sees an approaching Variable and shoves it out of his direction; turns back to see Nulo sprint across the arena. Opha mumbles to himself, "Coward!"

Nulo clears his throat for attention and yells, "You guys are in for a treat. Normally I just tease you all with one new move, but I'm feeling generous today. This next one has never been done or practiced before. It's called 'The JMI'. Why? Because I Just-Made-It."

Before Nulo starts, Lieutenant Kaphir shoves him. "Why don't you stop performing and help us?"

"I am helping. I'm making your job easier."

Kaphir leans closer. "We don't need help with fighting, I'm talking about your yapping mouth; shut it."

Nulo leans in and whispers, "You saying you don't need my help?"

"That's what I'm saying. And I'm sure everyone in here agrees."

Nulo tilts his head and smiles. "Ah come on, everyone needs a little help sometimes."

A desperate plea interrupts their conversation, "Can I get some help over here? I need ammo now."

Nulo pinches Kaphir's cheeks. "You see, buddy?" Nulo calculates the distance between the needy lieutenant and the responding officer. He darts ahead.

The officer sprints towards the lieutenant, toting a backpack full of ammo.

At the same time, Nulo kicks a Variable down, using it as a step to hurdle over a cluster of fighters. Nulo tackles another Variable into the officer, rolls on to his feet and snags the backpack. "I'll take it from here." He tosses formunition cartilages at the lieutenant and salutes the observant Kaphir.

The balcony goes wild once more. "Nulo, Nulo, Nulo!"

Nulo cups his hand around his ear for them to scream louder. "I can't hear you," Nulo shouts as he smiles and flexes his muscles for his admirers. "There's more to come," he promises. He turns and dives onto the back of a running Variable, dragging his knees and pulling it to the ground. He explains, "You, my friend, will be the chosen Variable that will make

13

headlines with me. Smile for the cameras." Nulo grits his teeth and strangles the creature in a headlock until it's motionless. "I hope they got my good side."

· ·

"Can you untie me please?" begs a bound and exhausted Rhoddy.

Grae shrugs. "Why?"

"Because I'm innocent. I have nothing to do with you or this guy Sultri."

"Oh yeah?" Grae squats in front of Rhoddy and holds up a digital image from his TDA. "Then why are you two in this image together?"

Busted, Rhoddy closes his eyes. "I can explain."

"Strike 25. Now it's time for the truth, huh?"

Rhoddy cries, "He paid me not to say anything."

"Oh, so *Sultri* paid *you* and not me? Oh this is just getting better and better."

"But it wasn't a lot. All he said was if anybody asks about him, I should just act dumb."

"Well, you're certainly doing a great job. I'm going to kill him."

"He's gonna pay you. I don't know when, but he said he had to pay off a debt."

Grae puts two and two together and presses his face against the booth window. He grabs a set of binoculars and scans the many lieutenant faces. "You better pray he's down there, because you are one too many lies over my patience."

Suddenly, they hear a booth page from an officer.

"Come in, Officer."

Grae looks at Rhoddy and tries to ignore the call.

Frowning, Rhoddy shrugs. "Obviously, I can't answer. Hurry up before they think something's wrong."

"Ugh." Grae rushes to the intercom. "This is Officer Grae. What do you need?"

"We have an escort down here that lost their boarding card. How do you want to handle this?"

Before pressing the intercom, Grae asks Rhoddy, "What would you do?"

"You're in charge. You have to give them another boarding card."

Grae presses the intercom. "Is it a girl or a guy?"

"I'm sorry. What was that?"

"You heard me, is it a male or a female?"

"The barter officer clears his throat and whispers, "It's a female, sir."

Grae asks, "Is she cute?"

The officer pleads, "Come on. Don't make me answer that. She's standing right in front of me."

"It will determine if it's worth me leaving my comfortable booth to fix the situation. Is she cute or not?"

Grae stares at the intercom for an answer and finally hears, "Never mind, sir. I'll figure something out."

Grae disconnects and Rhoddy yells, "I can't believe you just said that."

"Don't get me started on all the lies you've stirred up. I'm two seconds away from kicking you in the teeth."

Rhoddy shakes his head and pouts.

CHAPTER 2

Located directly below the mezzanine, is the lobby level, which rarely receives Variable disturbances. It is the more secured stadium and exclusively used by the Iotas. The Arvelee's commanders are hired to protect their priority packages coming on and off the ship. They are stationed at the rear of the stadium, covering the loading docks during the Iota's private transactions.

Commander Dena patiently lies on her stomach and observes the many exchanges through her binoculars. On the opposite side of the stadium, is her aggravated friend, Commander Locy. She whispers in her TDA to Dena, "Does your back hurt over there as much as mine? To top it off, I think I'm coming down with something." Locy sniffles, squirms for comfort and stretches her lower back. She squints toward the unresponsive Dena and rolls her eyes. "Since you're so busy ignoring me, I guess I can take a break now." Locy pushes herself up and begins to rotate her aiming wrist.

"Get back in position," Dena demands. "We're officially blind on your side."

Locy scoffs at her request. "Stop exaggerating. You know nothing happens down here."

"Yes, because the Iotas trust us and everyone knows what to expect."

"Well, I *expect* to work comfortably from now on. Who do we need to talk to, to get a softer platform over here? Like a roll out mat with some sort of memory foam."

Dena sighs and ignores her complaints, but Locy continues, "I can't be the only commander on board who feels this way. I should start a petition and ask around, huh? How's *your* back?"

"Shh," Dena whispers.

"Don't shh me. I'm asking out of concern for you. *Wouldn't* you like a memory foam platform?"

"My back is fine, okay?"

Locy folds her arms and mumbles, "Sometimes I just want to shoot her in the face."

"I heard that," Dena reveals. "Your radio is still on, genius."

Embarrassed, Locy clears her throat and quickly closes their connection.

Dena grabs her binoculars and notices an abnormal crate being rolled into the docks. She watches an opposing Iota solider stop the delivery from being loaded on board. Two other soldiers arrive and begin to corner the delivering soldier against his own crate. They ruffle his clothing and argue aggressively, pointing at the box. The accused solider pleads his case with confused shrugs and prayer hands.

Dena sighs and quietly radios Locy. "Heads up, looks like we might have a problem on Dock 3."

Locy reaches for her binoculars, but is met with a spell of dizziness. She holds up her wobbly head and attempts to regain focus. She is swarmed by soft whispering, haunting her from all directions. Locy flips to her hip and searches for the voices mocking and repeating her name. She begs, "No, no stop it. Why don't you just leave me alone?" She plugs her ears and vigorously tries to drown the internal badgering. The ghostly voices overlap louder with specific eerie demands. "Let go and lead us, Locy. Do not shun us. Listen!"

17

She rips opens her eyes and finds her body completely engulfed inside a painless, blurry, orange tint.

Again, she hears Dena calling, but this time muffled and distorted. "Locy, do you copy? Locy!"

"Yeah," she answers, low and uncertain. She is thrown into a strange trance at the sight of a dangling Leviathan staring down at her. Drool drips from the creature's open jaw and jagged teeth gnash under its snout. Frozen in place with rolling chills, Locy feels as if the idle beast is ripping her courage to pieces. Locy opens fire, but the recoil jerks her out of the hallucination. The shot hits the ceiling and rubble showers Dena's platform.

Dena points her AC up and searches the damaged roof. "What'd you see?"

Embarrassed, Locy stutters, "Umm, I thought I saw a Leviathan. You can never be too sure, you know? Sorry."

Dena reads Locy through her voice. "I don't have room for your *sorrys* or lies. Now tell me the truth."

Locy mumbles, "I'm sorry, my AC must've slipped."

"How many years have you used an arm cannon? They don't just *slip*. If anyone reports this, just make sure you have a better excuse than *'it slipped'*." Dena does a quick sweep through her binoculars to ensure everyone is safe down in the docks.

"Don't worry, those shady soldiers like to keep every transaction as secret as possible."

"You're not getting what I'm saying. You just opened fire in a stadium full of highly respected Iotas and our job is to protect them."

Locy chuckles. "Yeah, protecting them from getting exposed. Dena, there's a lot of dirt coming from the Beverod and our stubborn captain acts like she doesn't know what's going on."

Dena massages her forehead; aggravated by Locy's conspiracy. "Whatever."

"You see? You're doing it, too. You're ignoring everything wrong you see with the Iotas just like everyone else."

"Listen, what the Iotas do in private is not my problem. My only concern is following our law."

"Let me tell you where it all ties in..."

"No!" Dena says. "I don't want to hear so much as a sneeze from you until this shift is finished." Dena lies back down in position and switches channels to the barter officer up front. She toggles her TDA receiver and announces, "This is Commander Dena reporting an accidental bogie shot in your direction; please inform the clients everything is fine."

"Copy that and thank you."

Locy overhears Dena's announcement and yells across the stadium, "What was that all about?"

"Shh," Dena quickly responds over their shared channel. "Will you relax? I just covered both of our butts because I knew you weren't going to report your 'accidental' shot."

.   .   .   .

While he searches the crowd for Nulo, Opha grabs a Variable by its legs and uses it as a battering weapon against nearby Variables. Suddenly, Opha too is engulfed by a soft voice, *"It's time, Opha. We're living in the last days."* The voice continues to echo and he doesn't understand the meaning behind it. He becomes dizzy and starts to move slower in his daydream. He quickly falls out of the trance once a nearby lieutenant shoves him. "Give me a hand over here, O."

Opha fires four solid shots at his quarry, leaps up to a platform and hurdles over a railing. From the ground, the competitive Nulo snipes a Variable near Opha, winking at his shocked friend. Nulo yells, "Now we're even."

Opha holds his neck and frowns at Nulo's naiveté. He mumbles obscenities to himself as he watches Nulo prance away with a boastful grin. Opha wants to teach him a lesson. He climbs just below the balcony area and hides in the shadows of the bleacher doors. You want to play, Mr. Nulo? Let me show you what it feels like.

Opha reloads his AC with a full clip and searches the arena for Nulo. Through his scope, Opha sees Nulo charging two Variables. Opha hunts them both down with two direct shots. Nulo turns to see who stole his kill. He sprints toward another set of Variables a few feet away. Opha fires again. Nulo runs into nothing but Variable fragments.

"Hey," Nulo yells and looks for the thief.

Opha laughs at Nulo's discouraged expression and decides to leave him wondering. Opha comes out from hiding and makes his way back to the battleground. Opha's eyes widen when he sees an isolated Variable in the corner of the bleachers, ripping metal back and eating a hole through the insulation. "How did no one see you up here?" Opha whispers as he readjusts his sniper scope. Nulo sees the scoundrel, too, and climbs towards it to get a better shot. Opha locks onto the Variable's torso and fires.

Nulo slowly follows the path of the shot and shoulder tackles another Variable from the line of fire. He spins and releases his own shot. The Variable combusts.

"Why?" Opha yells as he leaps down from the platform. "Why must he be this way?" He pushes through the crowd of crossing lieutenants and finds Nulo chatting with Sultri. "Did you see that shot? Yeah, sometimes I surprise myself."

Lieutenant Sultri doesn't answer and instead shakes his head at Nulo's selfish performance. Opha arrives and Nulo says, "You thought I didn't know it was you stealing all my kills? No one in this arena, besides you, is dumb enough to play a game like that."

"Why is everything a competition with you?"

Nulo blows imaginary smoke off his palm barrel. "Once you get as good as me, there ain't no competition." Nulo turns to the eavesdropping Sultri and says, "No offense."

Opha points to what's left of the Variable and says, "Come on, you know I had a perfect shot."

"If it was perfect, it would have connected."

"I don't have time for your games. You can steal all the kills you want from your little fans around here, but don't touch mine."

Nulo instantly assumes Opha is below the required quota. If so, Opha will be ordered to attend the purging ceremony along with the bottom one percent of the ship. It's a division percentage that encourages diligence and keeps the healthier phages on board. Some soldiers return with a probation warning, while others are purged off the ship.

Nulo looks at his AC and sees his kill counter at 330. He has a bad feeling about Opha's number. He's ashamed of his selfish behavior, but even more, he is now worried for Opha's life.

. . . .

Haunted by the truth, Locy struggles to keep her mouth closed about what really happened earlier. She humbly looks at Dena and whispers, "Dee, I know you're probably still pissed at me, but hear me out really quick."

"What?" Dena mumbles.

"I want to tell you what I've been going through, so you don't think I'm going crazy."

"Oh, I'm beyond *thinking,* because you've proved it."

"In all seriousness, I want to try to explain." Locy sighs. "So... have you ever, like...um..."

"Spit it out. I don't have all day."

"Do you sometimes hear random voices telling you to do things?"

Dena drops her head. "Please don't make me answer this."

"I know what it sounds like, but I'm trying to give you the back story of my dizzy spells. I can't really describe it, because each time is different. A bunch of freaky things been happening to me and I want it to stop. Like this one time I lifted my shoes up with my mind, Dena. My mind!"

"Yup." Dena blurts, "You're crazy. You forced me to say it."

"I'm telling you the truth."

"Listen, whenever you start hearing *voices,* that's a given sign you're going crazy."

"My brother said he hears the same type of voices."

Dena laughs. "Your brother was a horrible example. Everybody knows he's a psycho."

"Yeah, but I really think we're onto something now because the evidence he recently showed me proves the Iotas are not who they appear to be. What I'm about to say has to stay between the two of us."

Dena answers with an exaggerated sigh.

"He said there's a secret Iota movement on the rise and we need to start planning a defense."

Shh, shh. Dena hears a faint channel frequency in her earpiece and quickly looks through her binoculars. "What was that noise?"

Locy slowly pans her assigned bartering section, but doesn't see anything out of the ordinary. "What did you hear?"

"Sounded like another conversation merging with our frequency."

Locy panics. "Oh no, I think they're on to me."

Dena demands, "Check under my post. I think something just crawled up under me."

Locy swings her binoculars and sees the cape of a shadowy figure.

"What do you see?" Dena asks.

Locy squints and begins to believe it's another hallucination. She drops the binoculars and boldly reports, "There's nothing down there."

CHAPTER 3

As the Extermination & Bartering Process comes to an end, Grae gets more frustrated with his intense search for Sultri. He asks, "Tell me the truth, where is your buddy hiding?"

Exhausted, Rhoddy says, "For the last time, Sultri said he'll be in the arena."

"To be totally honest with you, it's really difficult for me to believe anything you say."

"Then why are you asking me questions with the intention of not believing me?"

"Because I hope to catch you in another ridiculous lie so I won't feel so bad while I'm stomping your ribs into your lungs."

Rhoddy struggles to swallow. "I kind of wish I hadn't asked."

Grae walks back to the window and says, "Here's the deal. If I don't see Sultri before this shift ends, you're going to inherit his debt with interest."

"Whoa, whoa, whoa! What type of deal is that?"

"The type of deal that's rooted in the pool of lies you've created to cover him."

"I told you everything I know and I don't think it's fair at all."

"Whelp, that's life. And since you two are such good friends, you can just have Sultri pay you what I'm going to take from you."

"And how much is that?"

Grae smiles. "It was ninety, but now it's one hundred quota points."

"Come on, man," Rhoddy pleads. "It's my anniversary and I still haven't gotten my girlfriend a gift."

"Is that another lie?"

Ashamed, Rhoddy lightly nods.

"200 now! You're a liar without reason. Do you even have a girlfriend?"

"No."

"You're pathetic. I see why you and Sultri hang out together."

. . . .

Nulo does an unnecessary backflip off a wall, continuing to show off for the Iotas. He leaps over the shoulders of a nearby lieutenant and dives into a crowd of Variables. He lands on his knees, before leaping onto the back of a crawling Variable. He grabs ahold of its bushy mane and drags his heels to slow the raging beast. Nulo waves to his fans, releases his grip and suddenly incinerates the Variable's torso. He shimmies the ashes from his body and welcomes the applause. He nudges Sultri, who just so happens to be fighting nearby. "Did you see that last move?"

Sultri murmurs, "Yeah you made sure everyone saw it."

"Judging by your sarcasm, it almost sounds like you are *hating*."

Sultri raises his hands. "Busted."

"You're funny, but humor won't get you paid in here." He raises his eyebrows and passively pats Sultri on the head. Nulo jogs through the warfare and looks for his friend, Opha. He leans into his sight and asks, "Hey, O, did you see what I just did over there?"

Without looking, Opha answers, "No, but your audience made it clear you did something stupid."

"Stupid or amazing? Because I'm going with word, 'stu-mazing'. Ha, I should patent that before someone takes it from me, huh?"

"Whatever. I refuse to worship you or your *stupid* acts."

"Stu-mazing acts. Come on, O, help me brand this."

25

"Do me a favor and leave me alone." Opha checks his TDA and grunts at his Variable count. Nulo catches a glimpse of Opha's number as he walks away. Opha climbs the west ladder of the arena to join the sharp shooting lieutenants up top.

Nulo finishes off a few Variables and cautiously makes his way closer to Opha. "Hey, I'm sorry about that. You know I was just joking down there, right?"

"When did you start caring if you offended me or not?"

"You're my friend and I want to make sure we're in good standing."

"We're good."

Uncomfortably, Nulo searches for a segue. "Sooo, how's life?"

"What do you want?"

"I've seen your Variable kills and I don't want to see you in the next purging ceremony."

"Calm down, it's low, but it's not that bad."

"I seriously didn't know you were that far behind me. I would've never stolen that kill from you earlier."

"That was just one Variable."

"No. Each kill counts and the purging criterion doesn't care how good you are."

"Trust me, I'm fine."

"How many times have you been to the purging ceremony?"

"Once."

"That's one too many in my eyes. The Iota is always watching and trying to find any flaw to get rid of dead weight."

"One ceremony will not make or break me. And it's probably expunged from my records."

Nulo leans over and whispers, "Let's get you some kills."

Opha shoves Nulo out of his face. "I don't need your help."

"I'm not giving you anything; you're going to get them. Let's get you right before we clock out."

Opha slaps Nulo's hand off his shoulder. "Whatever you're thinking, don't include me in your show."

"I'm not showing off." Nulo swings the body of a passing Variable at Opha and he unintentionally blocks the flying Variable with a kill shot.

"What are you doing?" Opha yells.

"Getting you your quota without helping you. Follow me."

"No, I told you I don't..."

Nulo launches another Variable and Opha shoots it out of the air. "Will you stop throwing Variables at me?"

"Well, come on then." Nulo sprints forward switching to the stun formula on his AC and fires at a passing Variable. "Shoot him." The stunned Variable's body is frozen in place and Opha grunts at Nulo's plan. Reluctantly, Opha follows Nulo, disintegrating all the paralyzed Variables in their path.

Lieutenant Sultri witnesses Nulo aiding Opha and becomes furious. The resentful lieutenant gives an envious look to his surrounding crew who share his sentiment.

Nulo leaves a trail of numb Variables and exclaims, "Yeah, I set them up and you knock 'em down."

Opha catches a group of lieutenants pointing at Nulo and whispers to himself, "Now I'm the second most hated person on this ship." Opha glances at his kill count. "But I'll take free points any day." Opha reaches for the mace on his back to expedite the massacre. He demonstrates his strength and knocks out three Variables in one strike, screaming with every blow.

Lieutenant Kaphir rotates his shooting arm and decides to take a break. He finds his lighter in his cargos and flips the lid open. Before he could light his cigar, he gets hit in the elbow, throwing his lighter. He looks down at a severed Variable limb. "Watch it," Kaphir yells to Opha. He reaches down to pick up his lighter and realizes Opha and Nulo are working together. Kaphir repeats his warning, but Opha's victory cries drown him out.

The crowded balcony slaps the windows with a wave of cheering as the clock counts down. Opha gets caught up with the chanting and decides to alter his attacks. He performs a tornado spin while using his mace to quickly thrash a line of Variables. Opha spots a Variable crawling across the balcony's window. He aims through his scope, fires and annihilates the slithering creature. The elite cheer with raised hands. Nulo smiles at Opha. "Feels good, doesn't it?"

"What?"

"Don't act like you didn't purposely take that shot in front of the elite. Now they're all cheering your name."

Opha answers, "Ah, it's alright."

"Now you know how I feel. Just imagine hearing that every shift." Nulo glances at the barter clock, which is now under nine minutes.

Opha checks his kill count. "Just a few more and I'll be above average."

"Yeah, but I'm not average." Nulo choke slams two Variables at the feet of Opha. "Shoot 'em."

. . . .

28

Locy watches the clock on her TDA and counts down with the ticking seconds. As the alarm chimes, she recites with the announcement, *"Your shift is complete."* Locy pops up and sighs. "It's about time."

She rushes to the exit the stadium, but Dena shouts, "Wait."

Dena catches up with her and softly asks, "In all serious, are you in some sort of trouble?"

"No, why do ask?"

"Because you screamed, 'I think they're on to me' earlier and that kind of got me worried about you."

Locy waves it off. "Oh, it's nothing. Maybe my brother's conspiracy talk is wearing off on me."

Dena shrugs. "Alright, but we still can't leave until the next shift arrives."

"No Dee, I'm tired and I want to get out of here."

"This is not like the arena upstairs. It's just the two of us covering this entire level. And how many times have you been late for your shift? Exactly. Now stay on the clock and make these few extra quota points."

Locy laughs with sarcasm. "Pfft, you think I do this for points? I can make more points selling memory cards."

With Dena's back turned, Locy sees the shadowy image crawling on the wall again. She still doesn't know if it's real or not so she calmly asks, "Am I seeing things or is that a Variable?"

Dena spins around and sees the slithering creature as well.

"Thought so." Locy swings her AC in the direction of the Variable and fires.

Dena looks back at Locy. "I asked you earlier if you saw something under my post and you said no. Are you trying to get us fired?"

Still covering up her spell, Locy lies, "I swear to you I didn't see anything."

Dena calls a barter officer. "How did you guys let a Variable get this far back without notifying us? Now we don't know how long it's been feeding or the extent of damages."

An officer responds, "We apologize, Commander. It must've slipped through the sewers or something."

"Don't apologize to me; just make sure you file an incident report to Director Arooni as soon as your shift ends."

"Copy."

Dena tries to climb down to investigate, but Locy pulls her arm. "What are you doing?"

"I'm checking to see if the wall needs to be replaced or not."

"Let that officer deal with it. It's just going to give you more paperwork to fill out. And technically, we're not even supposed to be here. We're off, remember?"

"You're *so* not a team player."

"You are *so* right. I'm a smart player."

The elite officers wrap up transactions and head back to their respective ships. The lobby doors slowly crank close and the many soldiers use mag liners to deliver shipments to their rooms.

Shortly after, the second shift arrives. "It's about time, boys," Locy yells. "I don't care which one of you has it, but somebody is paying me 1000 quota points or I'm reporting your tardiness to a maphlete."

The late commanders fearfully look at each other and quickly divvy out the quota points from their TDAs.

. . . .

Opha waves a cloud of smoke away from his face and hurdles a tripped lieutenant, trying to keep up. He dangles from the lighting truss, firing a series of aerial shots while almost shooting Nulo in the torso. "Whoa!" Nulo looks up and shrugs.

Opha drops down and chuckles. "Sorry, I just got caught up in the moment."

"Apology not accepted, but I do take favors."

"For sure. I owe you."

"You ready?"

"For what?"

"This." Nulo takes off running and attempts his JMI move. Opha follows and watches him rush towards three Variables. Nulo rolls on the ground and catapults feet first from his shoulders, knocking two Variables to the ground before landing on his back. He then flips upward, wrapping his legs around a Variable's neck and heaving him towards Opha. Opha blasts it into ashes and asks, "What was that?"

Nulo points up to the screaming elite members. "That, my friend, is the reason why they sponsor me."

Opha scoffs and mumbles, "Cretchit, I fell right into that."

Nulo dusts his back off and winks. "Next time I'm going for six Variables." He flexes his biceps for his admiring fans.

Opha rolls his eyes. "Can we finish this shift like normal lieutenants? No more fancy moves or surprises."

Nulo spins back into action. "Being normal isn't me. Watch this." While trying to shoot over his shoulder, Nulo shoots Lieutenant Kaphir's leg. Kaphir screams and falls stiff holding his hamstring.

Nulo ducks and joins Opha behind a divider, hoping Kaphir didn't see who took the shot. Opha shakes his head and says, "That's what happens when you think you're bigger than you actually are."

Nulo snickers. "There aren't limits when it comes to Lieutenant Nulo."

"Now you're referring to yourself in third person?"

"Why not? They say I'm equivalent to three soldiers."

"Whatever." Opha spots a black, oddly built Variable with jagged scales poking out of his back. He follows the mutated creature with his eyes and throws a haymaker at its broad shoulders. The Variable slams into the wall, but does not disintegrate from his shot. Its open wound slowly depletes and regenerates back to normal. The Variable slowly stands and Nulo says, "We got a fighter on our hands, huh?"

"Wait," Opha says uncertainly. "That's not a Variable, it's a Leviathan." Opha scans the arena. "I hope it's the only one. Quick, let's report to the maphletes before more show up."

"No, wait. It'll be better if we take him down ourselves. We'll be heroes. All we have to do is combine and mix a few older formulas from our arm cannons. It's what the maphletes do, anyway." Nulo switches to his lowest formunition.

Opha says, "We don't have time for this. Look, that Leviathan is already ripping our ship apart."

"Yes because we're wasting time talking about. Come on, O."

"I can't help you on this one."

"Remember that favor you owe me? Whelp, I'm cashing it in now."

Opha sarcastically replies, "Of course you'd ask for it now."

Nulo laughs. "You in or not?"

"I'm in ... but only because I want to go beyond my quota."

"A Leviathan is worth at least twenty points. You will definitely get more than your quota."

Opha rolls his eyes. "Alright, let's get this over with."

Opha unloads several rounds in the Leviathan's face and chest while Nulo distracts and attempts to buckle its legs. Unaffected by the attack, it kicks Nulo across the arena.

Suddenly a second appears on the opposite side the arena. Opha yells, "Here comes another one!"

Nulo pushes up from the ground. "Ha, this shift just became fun." The second Leviathan immediately penetrates the arena's walls with its sharp claw, searching for nourishment.

Lieutenant Sultri sees the Leviathan breach and shoots one of them with a maph dart and reports, "This is Sultri. I have spotted a Leviathan on the mezzanine. Please send us the threat level and protocol as soon as possible, over."

A third and fourth Leviathan have now entered the arena. Nulo shouts, "Behind you!"

Opha ducks its reaching arm and yells, "This is getting out of hand." Nulo smiles and hooks his last clip of formunition under his AC.

Sultri catches up with the two and says, "I got maphletes on it, so leave the Leviathans alone until we receive their report."

"Sure thing, buddy." With no intentions of doing so, Nulo rudely pats and ruffles Sultri's hair.

Sultri narrows his eyes and growls at Nulo as he springs away.

Nulo pulls Opha aside and says, "Switch to your TCR-CD3. I'll hit him with my CD40 formula. I'm certain the combination will bring the Leviathans down. Start with the one on the far left."

"I think we should do what that lieutenant says and wait for the maphlete's instructions. Since there are four now, I'm pretty sure they're in the process of dropping a Nicil bomb."

"Just do it and stop being so scared. You're too big to be so soft."

Opha looks up at the cheering audience and hears them chanting his name. He starts to feel the pressure and abides, "I really hate you."

Nulo aims at the closest Leviathan. "You ready?" Opha nods and lifts his arm cannon as well. They open fire and surprisingly obliterate one of the four Leviathans.

Nulo jumps in the air. "Yeah! I told you I know what I'm doing. Don't ever doubt me." He looks at the shocked faces of his peers and says, "Who's the man? You ain't got to say it because we all know. Now do us all a favor and keep the Variables out of our way so Opha and I can take down the rest of these Leviathans."

Opha politely adds, "And he meant to say 'please', guys."

Lieutenant Sultri denies Nulo's request. "Don't help him. We all know he's a show off and we still haven't gotten word from the maphletes yet." Sultri's message triggers agreement and a retreat towards the exits.

Suddenly, all of their TDAs chirp at once. "Lieutenants, we've received word of a severe breed of Leviathans and we demand everyone to stand down, over."

Nulo's face lights up and he answers his TDA. "Esko, is that you? Hey, it's Nulo. Don't worry, Opha and I got everything under control." Nulo doesn't wait for a response and disconnects.

During the maphlete's instructions, three more Leviathans have slipped inside of the arena making a total of six. Opha watches them disperse and run rampant throughout the area. "There's just too many and not enough time."

"Opha!" the maphlete shouts. "Do you read me? If there's anybody near Nulo, tell him to turn his TDA back on and get out of there. We are about to drop the Nicil bomb."

Other lieutenants hear the mass announcement and begin to exit. Nulo ignores all the passing lieutenants and waves them goodbye. "Good, go ahead and leave just like he said. It only makes it easier for my fans to see us pull off this encore."

Opha starts to exit, but Nulo stops him. "Wait. Help me out with one last thing."

"No."

"Listen, the Nicil bomb won't be here for another five minutes. If we do this right, we can take down at least four and get out of here with time to spare."

"Are you crazy?" Opha tries to leave again.

"No. I've done this a thousand times. Are you finally going to let me die this time?"

Opha doesn't fall for Nulo's brandish trick. "Yes, because I'm leaving."

"Come on, let's make history." Nulo relies on the fact that Opha is easily influenced, gives him an eliciting expression and takes off towards the closest Leviathan. Opha watches Nulo run off. He looks at the exiting lieutenants and bites his knuckles. "I hate him, I hate him. Nulo, wait up."

. . . .

Confused, Grae skims the arena trying to make sense of the retreating lieutenants. He adjusts the knobs on his binoculars and luckily comes across Sultri. Grae carefully follows him leading the evacuation and whispers, "You're not getting away from me that easy." Grae packs his items and yells, "Looks like you're in luck, Rhoddy. I got eyes on your buddy, Sultri, in the arena."

Grae looks back to find Rhoddy has fallen asleep in the tape. He kicks the pole. "Hey!"

Rhoddy jumps from his slumber and knocks his head against the underside of the table. "What do you want now?"

"I was trying to tell you you're off the hook. I found Sultri."

Rhoddy looks to the ceiling and sees the silent red siren spinning. "Oh no. How long has that light been on?"

Grae shrugs. "I don't know, about ten minutes. Why?"

"Because the Nicil bomb has been dropped. We have to get out of here."

Grae grabs his bag. "That's all you had to say. See you around."

"Wait," Rhoddy screams. "You can't leave me tied up like this. I helped you find Sultri, didn't I?"

Hesitant, Grae slowly returns with a blade. "If I let you go, my name won't ever come out of your mouth, right?"

"I don't even *know* your name because you never gave it to me."

"You're not lying again are you?"

"No, and if it makes you feel better, I've never seen you before."

"That's the spirit." Grae slices the tape off Rhoddy and pulls him away from the pole.

Grae starts to climb out of the booth and Rhoddy yells, "Wait, can I have my arm cannon back?"

Grae smiles. "I don't trust you that much."

Rhoddy mumbles, "Jerk."

The arena is now crawling with Variables and Opha and Nulo are the Arvelee's only defense. The creepy zombiesque moaning from Variables, vibrate the aluminum walls of the mezzanine. Nulo zips through the slippery creatures, aims and shoots towards one of the Leviathans, misses, but Opha follows up with the kill shot. Nulo thanks him with a point and continues to orchestrate his nonsensical plan. He spots another Leviathan digging a hole under the staircase and darts forward. Nulo climbs, balances and runs off the backs of crouching Variables. He aims, but miscalculates a step and furiously twists his ankle.

Opha stops firing once he hears Nulo's long and agonizing scream. Nulo tightly holds his ankle and tries to stand, but is stampeded by a swarm of Variables coming from all directions. Opha pulls out his mace and swings a path towards Nulo's voice. He charges forward and tackles a sea of Variables, causing them to fall in a domino effect. Opha stands on top of the pile and locates Nulo as he tries to regain his balance. Opha bombards through and offers him a hand. "I'm here, come on."

He reaches for Opha's sweaty, slippery arm, but is unable to grab hold. His hand is slapped and kicked away by the Variables until Opha lunges forward and pulls Nulo up by his shawl. Nulo painfully grunts and limps behind Opha while shooting Variables in their path. Opha throws Nulo's arm over his shoulder and says, "We're done." Nulo agrees with a wink and misses a step. His injured foot gets tangled with Opha's and both fall to the ground, trampled beneath the mindless Variables.

38

The balcony audience starts to panic, but the bets are tripled for their survival. An Iota member screams, "45,000 q-points says they won't make it out alive." Others join in by throwing in quota chips. "I'll second those odds." The betting wars escalate as one of Nulo's sponsors stand in silence, watching the Nicil timer countdown.

Opha plants his feet and squats low to the ground with a forearm block; trying to find Nulo through the horde of legs. He pivots, but gets forcibly pounded on his hip. Opha's broad chin and ribcage is continuously smashed against the floor. He catches hold of Nulo's shoulders as he rolls by. "Get up. We don't have much time."

They use their weight as leverage and finally get back on their feet. The overwhelming storm of Variables continues to blindside the duo, pushing and shoving them apart. Opha punches a Variable with his mace and yells, "I can't see the exit, Nulo, aim towards the door." Nulo hops onto Opha's back and shoots over his shoulder. His tight grip unintentionally chokes Opha. Gagging, he asks, "What are you doing?"

"I'm making a path for us."

Opha struggles to talk. "I said shoot towards the exit, not use me as a chariot."

Nulo continues to fire. "Be a team player, I got a bad ankle."

"Let go of my neck. I want to still be alive when we exit." Opha continues to carry Nulo and hears his TDA.

"Get out of there now, do you hear me? I'm talking…" Nulo reaches over and turns Opha's radio off.

Opha is baffled. "What was that?"

"A bunch of nonsense. They clearly see us trying to leave. Why do we need to hear the obvious?"

Opha slows down. "They are going to think I cut them off. I'm blaming you for all of this."

"Yeah, they always do." The exit is steps away and Nulo hops off Opha's back and spins around. Opha pulls the exit hatch. "Come on, what you are doing?"

Nulo nods. "I'm coming." The upper pipes echo and shake from the distant sound of the Nicil approaching. Nulo backpedals with a limp and sees the frenzied Variables crawling from the roof to the walls and playfully says, "I just need to find that perfect stu-mazing shot before I go."

He lightly waves Opha away and searches through his cannon scope. Nulo, dancing along with his chanted name, licks his lips in preparation. The brave lieutenant fires, but is distracted by the sudden clangorous missile arriving above.

He fails to hit his target. "Cretchit." He swiftly exits, but hears Iota voices booing him behind the door. Nulo reenters the arena, exposing the ship and aims high. "Never doubt my encore." He fires blindly and immediately locks and slams the door shut. Nulo leans his weight and feels the violent quake erupt on the other side. His single shot soars through the smoke, parallel to the Nicil, and strikes a feasting Variable across the arena.

BOOM. The Nicil bomb explodes, and wipes out every living being in the arena.

The audience covers their eyes from the blinding blast and cheers abundantly. The balcony winners quickly divvy up their earnings and cash them into quota points.

The exhausted lieutenants safely watch the level lights flicker from outside the sealed doors and begin to celebrate. Nulo checks his TDA for his last shot and gives himself a silent fist pump as it clicks up ten more points. "Nice."

CHAPTER 4

Commander Locy slouches across from Dena, watching as she massages her neck in the empty locker room. Dena unscrews a pink pill bottle and throws a capsule down her throat. She looks across at Locy and asks, "Why aren't you taking your vaccine pills? It's time."

Locy shrugs nonchalantly.

Dena lifts Locy's dropped chin. "You can't play like this. They are called vaccine pills for a reason."

Locy walks away and inspects the aisles of the locker room to ensure their privacy. She prances back to Dena and sits beside her. Locy holds the pink bottle up and whispers, "I think the pills are fake."

"Why?" Dena asks.

"Because I haven't taken one pill in the past month and I don't have any signs of Variablitus."

Dena inhales, stunned. "You really are trying to kill yourself, aren't you?"

"No. There've been a few rumors floating around about the side effects and I wanted to see if they were true."

Dena yells, "Your health is not a game of trial and error. Just do what the Iota say and take the pills."

"Shh," Locy hisses. "Keep it down. We don't know who is listening. Just hear me out. Have you ever heard of one story of a soldier getting sick from Variable contact?" Dena takes a moment to think about it and realizes she hasn't. She turns away from Locy and sucks her teeth. "You see?" Locy nods her head in response to Dena's silence.

Dena responds with uncertainty, "But we don't know everything. We don't know what the Arvelee has done to prevent that. Some things will just never be answered."

"And that's the problem with this ship. Everyone is either too afraid or too lazy to ask the Iota anything." Dena sits down to reload her arm cannon and thinks about her own unanswered questions. All of a sudden the entire room shakes and lights flicker from above.

Locy begins to glow in a fluorescent orange and the ghostly voices return. The lockers begin to rattle and swing open as Locy violently controls them with her emotions. "Dena," Locy yells. "Are you seeing this?" Unresponsive, Dena guards her head and curls up in a fetal position.

The paranormal experience stops and Locy yells, "Did you feel that?"

"Of course I did. It's the aftermath of a Nicil drop upstairs."

"No," Locy says. "It wasn't, it was me. I controlled the entire room with my mind. Just like I was telling you earlier."

Dena shrugs. "I don't know what to tell you. I guess that'll be another unanswered Iota question."

Locy cries out, "You think I'm crazy, don't you?"

"I didn't say that, you said it."

"But you were thinking it." Locy removes a stack of files from her locker and shoves the mysterious papers into her backpack. She mumbles out loud and cries with her back turned.

Curious, Dena asks, "What were those papers?"

Locy zips the bag. "It's none of your concern now."

"Whatever you're planning on doing, think about the consequences. Talk to me. I'm still your friend and don't want to see you hurt."

Locy hears a knocking pipe and lowers her voice in a panic. "Shh, come on." Locy leads Dena out of the locker room and down the hall. They enter a secure stateroom and she slams the door shut.

. . . .

Nulo limps through the throng of lieutenants and patronizes them individually. He offers fist bumps and encourages flimsy high-fives. "Good job. Great job, my friend. As a matter of fact, all of you were on the top of your games and I really mean it this time."

He wobbles over to Opha and whispers, "That's how you put on a show."

Embarrassed, Opha asks, "How do you keep pulling me into dumb stuff?"

Nulo lifts up Opha's TDA and shows him the 490 quota points on the screen. Nulo clears his throat. "You were saying?"

Opha stares at Nulo with a stone cold expression, but slowly smiles.

Nulo grabs Opha and puts him into a playful headlock. "That's my boy."

. . . .

Locy whips out a portable debugger and scans the four corners of the room, searching for tracking devices. Dena follows close behind and asks, "What is going on?"

Locy shoves the debugger back into her book bag and says, "I want to show you why we shouldn't trust the vaccine pills or anything coming from the Iota." Locy searches her bag and pulls out the stack of papers. "I found documents that confirm the Extermination & Bartering Process is just to keep us distracted. It's not about shared resources or exterminating Variables; it's a mind-controlling event to keep us happy with quota points."

44

Dena grabs the stack of papers from her. "That's impossible."

"Is it? As smart as Captain Lyme is, don't you think she would've come up with a more preventable way to keep the Variables out, rather than using lieutenants and commanders? She hasn't. Instead, she lets the ship Beverod come up with this sick sport we agreed to."

Dena shuffles through the papers and sees supporting information. "There must be some sort of explanation for this. Have you tried to talk to the captain?"

"Are you brainwashed, too? There's no need to because we have the evidence." Irrational, Locy screams, "Now it's time we start a revolution and expose them all. We should spread the word and take back our ship tonight."

"Calm down," Dena says softly. "This is just circumstantial evidence and nothing has been proven. You're not thinking straight. Let's head up to my condo, think it over and try to plan this out perfectly."

Locy grunts. "You see? Now you're dismissive like this whole ship. You think I'm crazy?"

"No, you're just moving too fast with little evidence."

"I showed you, you read it yourself. I've seen all I need to see. Don't you want to know what the Iota is covering up?"

"Listen," Dena calmly says. "Have you considered that the voices and images you've been having *are* caused by Variablitus? It makes sense, right? You said you haven't been taking your vaccine pill for over a month."

Locy sucks her teeth in response to Dena's opinion. "You know what? Forget I said anything. I wish I never opened my *crazy* mouth, but for some reason I just thought you would be different." Locy begins to leave.

"Wait."

Locy zips up her bag and whispers, "Just make sure this doesn't leave the room. Nobody will ever believe you and you'll end up crazy like me." She leaves without another word.

Dena stands behind the door in a daze.

. . . .

Nulo searches his pockets for a resuscitation card and realizes he's all out. He checks with Opha. "Do you have any resus cards on you? I'll pay you back once we get to the pharmacy."

"How about you just go to the pharmacy now and get yourself a dozen. I know you have the quota points."

"Because my ankle is the size of your head and the closest one is at the nose of the ship. Cretchit. Why don't you ever have resus cards?"

Opha laughs and pulls out a jar. "Because I'm old fashioned. I prefer the cream over those cards."

"Yuck." Nulo pushes the jar away. "Get that out of my face. That stuff smells like feet and earwax!"

The automatic purge announcement lights up every screen located on the Arvelee. The mezzanine fills with phages gathering around the wall television; praying they don't see their names on the monitors. A digitized female's voice sounds over the intercom. "Welcome to the Purge Ceremony. We've calculated your Variable kills and the bottom one percent will soon be judged. Good luck." Hundreds of names are revealed. Phages throughout the ship react to their misfortune. The safe lieutenants shake hands and part ways with friends and soldiers.

Nulo salutes an under-achieving lieutenant walking by. "Maybe next time, huh?" Opha shoves Nulo. "Come on, have some integrity."

"What did I do?"

"Show some compassion and be a role model for once."

"I am a role model by just being Nulo. I consider myself the template of the Arvelee soldier."

"You are unbelievable."

"The word is stu-mazing, remember? Stu-mazing. Marketing."

Opha walks away, shaking his head.

.   .   .   .

Dena helplessly curls up in a corner of the stateroom and weeps for a sense of direction. She looks around the room and spies an outdated computer covered in plastic. She kicks over a small ottoman to sit on and rips off the plastic protector. Dena logs on using her credentials and begins her own research. "I'm sorry, Locy, but I have to get to the bottom of this." Dena pulls up a training module diagram of the Arvelee and saves it to a memory card. She scans the table of contents, clicks on "origin" and begins to read through any document that seems helpful.

She discovers the buried Beverod files, but cannot select them for some reason. For every attempt she makes to open the folders, a rejection window appears. Dena mumbles, "This so weird." She shuts down the computer and voice activates information from her TDA. "Find me the latest Beverod treaty with Division 5."

.   .   .   .

47

"Wait up," Nulo yells while limping behind Opha. "You know I still have this bad ankle."

Nulo trips into a group of chatting soldiers and breaks up their huddle.

A female lieutenant aggressively turns around. "Watch it, moron." When Lieutenant Nushaka realizes it is Nulo, she quickly adjusts her tough demeanor. "Oh hey. Had I known it was you, Lieutenant, I wouldn't have been so rude. Great job in there."

Nulo rotates his ankle. "Thank you, ladies."

Nushaka snickers. "My girls and I were just talking about you and were going to look for you. So listen, a few of us are starting a fighting league and thought it would be more competitive if we divided ourselves into teams. That way it doesn't feel like we are just killing Variables for the Iota's entertainment."

Disinterested, Nulo interrupts, "That sounds like a whole lot of fun, but I'm in desperate need to get my ankle repaired at the pharmacy. But let's hook up later, okay?" Nulo leaves Nushaka without allowing her to answer.

He catches up with Opha, who's arguing with the contentious Kaphir. "Perfect," Kaphir proclaims. "Just the two lieutenants I've been looking for."

Nulo looks at Opha befuddled. "What is it?"

Opha mumbles, "Lieutenant Kaphir wants us to apologize."

"For what?"

"He's the guy you accidently shot in the arena. I tried to apologize *for you*, but he wants to hear it from you."

"That's it? All you want is an apology?"

Kaphir nods, "Yeah. I'm just putting it out in the open so you know I was aware of what happened."

"Well, I'm sorry." Nulo folds his arms and shrugs. "Is that it?"

Kaphir grinds his teeth at the apathetic apology and digs deeper. "Are you being sincere?"

"No. Is that sincere enough for you Lieutenant *Eye Patch*?"

Opha steps between the two, and says, "Just say you're sorry so we can put this behind us.

"I already did. Do I have to say it again so his good eye can catch it? I'm sorry, I'm sorry. Happy now?" Nulo bumps into Kaphir's shoulder and storms away.

Opha tries to soften the blow. "He really is sorry. We had a crazy shift and you just caught him at a bad time. Are we good?"

Kaphir clenches his jaw and nods his head slightly. "Yup."

"Thanks. Guess I'll see you around." Opha shakes Kaphir's hand and chases after Nulo. Kaphir says to the empty hallway, "He has no idea what he's gotten himself into."

Opha shoves Nulo and whispers, "What was that?"

"It's called honesty. I'm sick and tired of everyone thinking I owe them something. Do you want to know what I'm really sorry for? The lack of ambition in these so-called soldiers. The pity parties and quick favors they want from me. That's what I'm sorry for."

"But you're Nulo. You attract attention. What do you expect from them?"

"Are you taking their side?"

"There's no side to take. They're your fans."

"I get that. All I'm saying is, they should be more respectful with what they ask of me."

49

"Do you understand you are nothing without them? If you learn to appreciate your admirers, they will learn to respect you." Opha notices Sultri waiting behind Nulo and adds, "And you can start right now."

Nulo turns around and sees the grinning Sultri. Nulo exhales and reluctantly asks, "How can I help you?"

Sultri extends his hand and says, "Great job in there, seriously."

"Thank you, buddy. Oh hey, you were the one who fired off the maphlete dart right?"

"Yes I was, sir."

Nulo bows dramatically. "What you did in there was very brave. If it wasn't for you, Opha and I probably wouldn't have gotten out alive."

"Thank you." Nulo gives Opha a smug look and starts to walk away. Sultri quickly steps in front of him. "While I'm here, I need to ask you a question. More like a favor."

Nulo vulgarly exhales. "I'm sorry, Lieutenant...um?"

"Sultri, Lieutenant Sultri."

"Soupy." Nulo mispronounces Sultri's name and says, "Can we do this some other time? I need to finish my conversation with Opha. I'll catch up with you later, okay?"

Sultri is insulted by the swift rejection and forces an accepting smile. "Sounds like a plan."

Opha and Nulo walk towards the pharmacy. Opha says, "I can't be associated with your negative energy. I'm a good person and I know deep down inside you are, too."

"What makes you think I'm not a good person? I'm sorry, let me reword that, the best person?"

"Because you're saying arrogant things like that. Your enemies will start becoming my enemies and I can't risk it."

"Don't you get it? As long as I'm doing something right, I'll always have enemies. So why try to win everyone's blessing?"

Opha throws his hands up. "I give up on you."

"Yeah, yeah because you're a quitter!" Nulo shrugs and lets Opha walk away. He heads to the pharmacy to finally treat his ankle. While in line, someone yells his name.

"Nulo!"

"What now?" He slowly turns around to face a nametag. Nulo looks up inside the breathing nostrils of Maphlete Ghii and pats his broad chest. "Heeeeey, big buddy, good to see you again."

Ghii quickly clamps down on the back of Nulo's neck and yanks him before he can say another word. "Ah! Watch the ankle." Ghii tightens his fingers and walks Nulo down the hallway, as Nulo's red face is on display for all passing pedestrians.

Nulo tries to make small talk with a cheap insult. "So where's our one-legged friend, Esko, hiding?" Ghii doesn't respond and pushes Nulo towards the exit.

CHAPTER 5

Dena casually scans the network on her TDA's touchscreen and selects a folder. As the content loads, Dena gets up and opens the stateroom door, but doesn't see anything interesting in the hall. She leaves the door open and pulls her hair back into a ponytail in front of a nearby vanity mirror. Dena wipes her cheeks, and catches a glimpse of an unfamiliar reflection as it shoots past the mirror. Dena spins around and yells, "Hello?"

Dena reaches for her belt and loads a full cartridge of formunition in her AC and pursues the intruder. She hears faint footsteps running south and she cautiously peeks before entering the hallway. With sweat forming at her brow, she thrusts her AC in front of her with a slight tremble. She moves carefully along the hallway, clears her throat and demands, "Who's there?"

Dena hears distant laughter from pedestrians, but nothing in her vicinity. She takes a few more steps down the dimly lit hallway, before flicking on her flashlight. Dena hears a clang and sees a phage swiftly running towards a dead end.

"Stop," Dena commands, "Identify yourself at once."

With his hands up, a peculiar-looking phage slowly walks from behind the ship's shutter and shouts, "Don't shoot, I am Officer Riti."

"Officer? What are you doing on the lobby level without clearance or a proper escort?" Dena asks with her arm cannon pointing at his chest.

The officer blinks uncontrollably, triggering Dena's suspicion. He stares at her aimed AC and stutters, "I-I got lost circulating with, uh, the barter escorts through that last Nicil bomb evacuation."

"Interesting," Dena says, seeing through his lie. "Because there's no access to the lobby level from the bartering facilities." Dena slams the officer against the wall. "Don't lie to me! Now are you following me because of Locy?"

"Who? No."

Dena shoves her rifle into his neck and asks, "Then why are you snooping around?"

"Alright, alright. I'm a stowaway, okay? I'm just a runaway from the Ship Amyn from Division 11."

Dena flips Riti over her shoulder and onto the ground, "Are you done lying? Because you are only making me angrier."

Dena kneels on Riti's neck and watches as he squirms for air. "I'm not lying. I'm telling you the truth."

Dena slowly releases her pressing weight and asks, "How did you make it here from Division 11?"

Riti holds his tender neck and says, "I'll show you." He stands and removes an image card from his TDA. Suddenly, Dena watches the Arvelee birthmark shift into the Amyn's. Dena snatches the card from his hand and points her AC at his head. "Where did you get this?"

Riti swallows. "From the Cove of the Amyn."

"Cove? What is that?"

"It's just a code word everyone's been using for the black market. It's a secret store that sells things from the Beverod that you can't find from the ship's pharmacy."

Dena pushes his back against the wall and asks, "If all of this is true, why did you run and then lie to me?"

Riti shrugs. "I've been on ships where soldiers fire first and ask questions later."

Dena hears chatter from distant soldiers and pulls him down the hallway. "Don't say another word." She pushes him into the stateroom and closes the door behind them.

. . . .

Nulo is catapulted through a doorway and lands inside an interrogation room. Ghii follows, dragging Nulo by his tender ankle to the only seat in the room. He cries out as Ghii slams him into the isolated seat. "All this isn't necessary. The arena is safe and no one got hurt."

"Shut up," Ghii shouts, spraying saliva into Nulo's face. He holds his earpiece and says quietly, "Yeah, I got him in inquiry suite 2A. Alright, copy that."

Ghii combs his bushy beard and smirks as he exits the room.

Nulo shrugs. "You really think holding me in a bigger room will be any different? Ha." He stands up and struts over to the mirrored wall. "Hmm, this is new." Nulo knows he's being watched and starts to make disturbing faces. He cups his hands around his eyes to see through the two-way mirror and mumbles, "Hello." Nulo limps over to a second door and turns the knob. Locked.

"Nulo," An overhead bullhorn blares, which causes him to fall to the ground.

He looks to the ceiling and mutters, "Hey, random voice."

"Sit down and shut up."

Nulo comically looks at himself sprawled on the ground. "Ha, looks like I beat you to it."

The doors swing open and several maphletes march in unison inside the room, creating a walkway. They salute Maphlete Esko as he storms inside. He enters between the lines of maphletes with a hood covering his eyes, Maphlete Ghii right on his heels. The linoleum floor scrapes with every other step, due to Esko's metal prosthetic leg. Esko sighs. "Why do you insist on being a one man army?"

Nulo struggles to his feet. "Hey fellas, long time no see."

"Answer the question."

Nulo raises his eyebrows and says, "Maybe I am a one man army. Some phages are just born to be legendary, you know." Esko signals for two maphletes to rough up Nulo. One restrains Nulo's arms and another punches the lieutenant in the ribcage. The strikes knock the wind out of him. Nulo grunts and asks, "What's that for?"

One of the maphletes picks Nulo up and slams him back in the chair. Esko explains, "Things have changed, my friend, and it's time for you respect me and my ranking."

Nulo smiles as he sits back in the chair and crosses his legs. "Listen, all this has been blown out of proportion. And like I said before, no one got hurt. We destroyed three Leviathans without the maphlete's help, Esko. If you ask me, I think you should be thanking me for the high ratings with the Iota."

"A thank you?" Esko shouts. "Are you kidding me?"

"Listen, if the maphletes would start trusting me, we would not have to drop so many Nicil bombs every year."

"So you have all the answers, huh? You know all the ship secrets and keep them all to yourself? I'm sick of you not giving me the respect I deserve as your superior."

Nulo checks his pockets and grins. "I think I'm all out of respect. But I'll make sure to RSVP to your next pity party."

Furious, Esko grips his staff and strikes Nulo across the jaw without warning. Stunned by the impact, Nulo chokes out an unintelligible expletive and doubles over.

Esko pulls Nulo upright and whispers, "Who do you think you are? You think you're invincible or better than me?"

"I don't know what you are talking about."

Esko gut punches Nulo once more. "That's it. I'm done playing games. I tried to reason with you, but you've forced my hand."

Nulo turns and spits a mouthful of blood onto the linoleum. "Yeah, yeah I've heard this speech before. You're no different than the rest."

"The difference is, I'm going to break you in so many ways, you're gonna beg to be purged." Nulo mock shivers. "You got me shaking in my boots."

A nearby maphlete hands Esko a clipboard and he reads off the crime counts, "Lieutenant Nulo, you will be charged and punished for negligence, irresponsible actions, insubordination and treason."

Nulo jumps to his feet. "Whoa, treason? Now you're just adding stuff."

Esko immediately kicks Nulo back into his seat. "It's the truth. You've jeopardized the ship, lured Lieutenant Opha into your conniving scheme and dismissed a superior's direct order."

"But no one got hurt!"

"Why do you cross the line of every rule on this ship?"

Nulo scratches his nose and mumbles, "At some point we all gotta cross that line to know how far we can go."

Esko quickly shoves his walking staff up to Nulo's neck. "So that's your thing, huh? Crossing lines?" Esko grabs Nulo's stubbled chin and squeezes his lips shut and yells, "Y'all hear that? My buddy here likes to cross lines. Okay, let's see if I can think of a couple to cross."

Nulo pulls his face free from Esko's grasp and says, "Like what?"

"You will be stripped of your rank immediately and assigned to train the officers for the upcoming bartering program. Maphlete Ghii, please do me the honor of deactivating Nulo's AC and removing all cards from his TDA."

"Whoa, hold on Esko." Nulo jumps up and two maphletes grab his arms following Esko's instructions. He squirms while Ghii injects a deactivating mechanism that reprograms Nulo's arm cannon. Helplessly, he pleads, "The bartering program? Don't you think that's over the top?"

Esko moves extremely close to Nulo's ear. "I'm just trying to find a way to break you."

"Well, good luck with that because once my sponsors find out I'm not in that arena tomorrow, they're going to have your head on a platter."

"That's your leverage? You think you can do and say whatever you want and just hide behind the Iota? Well I'll make sure I relay the message to them personally and suffer my fate."

"This is your idea of crossing the line? Embarrassing me and trying to make me an example?" "Yeah, because all the warnings didn't do the trick."

Nulo shakes his head. "If this ship falls apart, just remember it was your fault. Y'all hear me? If the Arvelee sinks, it's all because of this leader you call Esko." Ghii pulls Nulo from Esko's face and Nulo reminds them, "I'm the best thing that ever happened to this ship."

Ghii turns to Nulo. "That's enough talking. Shut up before you get yourself in more trouble."

Ghii and Esko head towards the exit, but Nulo quickly grabs Esko's hood. "You sure you want to do this?"

Esko smacks Nulo's hand away. "You brought this on yourself. And when it's over, I will have the pleasure of having the Arvelee's hero groveling at my feet; begging for his life back."

Nulo spits in Esko's face. "Good luck with that."

Esko wipes the froth off his cheek and departs. "Godspeed, old friend."

Ghii firmly taps Nulo's cheek and says, "You spit on me and I'll break your jaw in six places." Ghii flicks his eyebrow and struts through the line of maphletes. He exits the suite and runs into Esko still wiping off his face.

Esko balls up the soaked handkerchief. "We're going to break him for sure."

Ghii inhales deeply and looks back at Nulo through the window. "Are you sure about all this?" "Trust me, it's gonna work."

"This is Nulo. You know he doesn't break that easy."

"Just remember the plan. I guarantee it'll work." They exchange a confirming look and shake hands.

Ghii heads in the opposite direction and is rushed by Sultri, who was waiting in the hallway. Sultri clears his throat and asks, "Maphlete Ghii, can I have a moment of your time?"

Ghii sighs. "Is it urgent?"

"Sort of. It's about your friend, Nulo."

Ghii rolls his eyes and begins to walk with Sultri trying to keep up. Ghii asks over his shoulder, "And what has he done to you?"

"Nothing. Actually, it's hard to explain."

"Well, get to it, Lieutenant, I got things to do."

"It's concerning the favoritism that's being displayed towards Nulo. I'm uncomfortable fighting with him on the same arena level."

"You are speaking with the wrong department. I can't help you."

"I spoke to some other lieutenants and we all feel it's not fair that Nulo continues to receive major sponsoring with his over-qualified experience and his refusal to upgrade to another position."

"How is that affecting you again?"

"Because I want to succeed and be acknowledged for my work. If he stays a lieutenant, I will be overlooked and forever in his shadow."

Ghii chuckles. "To be honest, I've never seen you before. And saying you're in Nulo's shadow is a stretch."

"That's what I'm saying. Because of Nulo, no one knows how good I actually am."

Ghii stops, pulls out a tablet and looks at Sultri's nametag. "Let's take a look, Lieutenant." Sultri smiles at Ghii's sudden compassion. Ghii shakes his head and announces, "It says here you average about ninety kills per shift, you've dropped below the required purging percentage once, and you were late for your shift today."

Sultri cringes. "I can explain."

"Save it. I don't have time. Maybe you should work on you first, before worrying about Nulo. But now that he's gone, you have a good chance of getting your wish. Keep working."

"What do you mean he's gone?"

"Just do what I said. Good things come to those who have patience."

Maphlete Ghii walks away, leaving him alone in the hallway.

. . . .

Riti is seated on the ottoman, explaining his travels to Dena. She stands over his shoulders and quietly says, "I need for you to tell me everything."

"Okay."

Dena pulls the curtains closed. He jumps and scratches his ear as if something bit him.

"Are you okay?" she asks.

"Yeah. I've just been through a lot these past couple days."

Dena opens a bottle of water and takes a gulp. "Are you alone here?"

"Yes, and if you let me go, I'll be off this ship on the next barter."

"What's the rush? You have anything to worry about as long as you're telling the truth." He nods his head, but says nothing. Dena confiscates and inspects the items hidden on Riti. "How did you get this barter map of the Arvelee?"

"Like I said, from a Cove inside the Amyn."

"You sure you didn't steal this here? Only a few maphletes have access to these types of things."

"Yes, I'm sure, Commander."

"This is confidential information about my home ship that shouldn't be in the hands of a pirating officer."

"I understand completely, but for the right price anyone can get ahold of anything."

Dena says to herself, "The Cove?" She taps her fingers on the table and then paces with her arms folded. "So, you pirate a lot?"

"Yeah, I've been jumping ships almost four years now."

Dena starts to loosen up with the idea of travel and asks, "So you can leave the ship at your own will?"

"Yeah."

"Can you tell me what it's like?"

"It's different every time. It feels like every ship is a new vacation."

"I must say, I've never imagined life outside this ship before."

"Yeah, that's what the ship upkeep is for. To keep you living in luxury with no reason to leave."

Dena starts to see the connection to Locy's enslavement theory. She folds her arms and asks

Riti, "So why did you leave?"

He shrugs his shoulders. "I was just curious to see what the other ships were like."

"Now I am curious."

He points to a memory card on the table and says, "See for yourself. I scanned a lot of images."

Dena hurries to the table and scrambles to insert the memory card into her own TDA. She slides through the touchscreen of images. "Wow."

Riti smiles and walks to the curtain to check his surroundings. "I know, beautiful, huh?"

"Yes."

"Trust me; they're not all so grand. You definitely run into some slummy layovers and toxic ships."

Dena closes her eyes and imagines. "Just the option of leaving the ship is blowing me away."

"It's forbidden information that city ships refuse to share with their phages. All Captains agree it is for the best."

"But why?"

"Loyalty. It's a controlling tool to keep you on the team."

Dena scratches her head in disbelief. "You're the second person today that mentioned something like this. What's happening on these ships that's such a secret?"

"I would tell you if I had an easy way to explain it, but I'm still searching for answers myself."

"Are you a rebel or a fugitive or something?"

Riti laughs and sits back down with confidence. "Fugitive? With all due respect, Commander, I'm free."

He realizes she doesn't fully comprehend his statement. "Listen, I know this ship is your home and all you've ever known, but this isn't it. It took several deaths for me to realize that life is bigger than just fighting Variables."

A forceful knock on the door startles the two. "Dena, are you still in there?"

It's Locy. Dena looks at Riti, puts her index finger over her lips and says, "Yes, what's up?"

"Why is the door locked? Open up."

"Hold on!" Before Dena can react, Riti grabs her arm. Dena silently gestures to him that she'll handle it. She unlocks the door and cracks it enough to talk.

"What are you doing?" Locy asks.

"Uh, I'm checking the breakdowns for tomorrow on the computer so I'll be prepared."

Locy detects that Dena is withholding information from her so she peeks into the room and sees Riti ducking inside. "I knew it." Locy bursts inside the stateroom. She points to Dena's face and says, "Busted. I knew you secretly had someone in your life; acting like you didn't have time for men."

Dena explains to Riti, "This is a misunderstanding."

Locy turns to Riti smiling. "Hi, I'm Locy, Dena's best friend and you are?"

Dena intercepts Locy's handshake. "No one." Dena then turns to Riti and explains, "I'm sorry, she was just leaving." Dena redirects Locy's shoulders and pushes her back towards the exit and whispers, "I'll explain later."

Locy whispers back, "No need to, I knew all along, Ms. Sneak-a-Dena."

"It's not like that."

Locy crosses her arms. "Oh, so you always sneak random men in private staterooms and lock the door?"

"Trust me, I will explain more when he gets done – I mean when he finishes – uh, when I get what I want...never mind, just leave, please."

Locy laughs out loud. "Okay, but at least tell me his name."

"Bye, Locy." Dena slams the door and takes a deep breath of relief. She gathers herself, turns around to see an open window and an empty room. Dena dives toward the window, but sees no signs of Riti. Dena checks the table and notices he has taken all of his items, but left behind the memory card. Dena logs off the computer and runs out of the stateroom.

. . . .

Sultri stomps down a heavily crowded corridor and hisses about his degrading day. He rudely pushes through soldiers, barely holding back his anger. "Move, move. Just get out of my way." To make matters worse, Sultri is tackled and driven against a door. He struggles to see who's responsible for the assault and gets his face shoved up to the peephole. Sultri strains to look over his shoulder and recognizes Grae. "Oh, hey!"

"Don't 'hey' me. Do you have any idea what I've been through to find you? You said you'd meet me in the barter booth."

Sultri gasps. "Whoa, calm down. What's gotten into you? It's me."

As a crowd begins to form, Grae feels the need put on his tough guy persona. Grae yells, "And that's the problem, I've been way too nice about my points and it's time for you all to take me seriously."

Confused, Sultri says, "You're hurting my arm."

Grae leans in and whispers, "Just go with it, I got other customers watching us and I want them to be afraid of me." Grae pulls back and yells, "Now, where are my points?"

Sultri plays along. "Uh, I'm sorry, Grae. I was gonna call you when I got all of it."

"And did you get it all?"

"Huh?"

Fed up, Grae slams Sultri's head against the door again. "You *heard* me. You're doing exactly what I said not to do, which doesn't compute as taking me seriously. Now I'm going to ask you one more time, do you have my ninety quota points or not?"

"Yes, yes I got them. I'll transfer them over as soon as you let go of my arm."

Grae looks at the watching bystanders and winks. "Good!" He calmly releases Sultri and whispers, "Meet me back in my cabin. And thank you for this."

CHAPTER 6

From the interrogation suite, Nulo is dragged aggressively to the hallway by two maphletes. They purposely disrespects Nulo's injured ankle by pushing and bouncing him back and forth. The shorter maphlete jokingly trips Nulo to aggravate his ankle even more. The maphletes snicker to one other as he reacts in pain.

"Cretchit," Nulo grumbles. "Hey Eyebrows, can you tell your Pint-Size buddy to chill out?"

The appalled, thick uni-browed maphlete yanks Nulo and asks, "What did you call me?"

Nulo shrugs. "Eyebrows, that's your name, right? And your robust, minuscule friend here is Maphlete Pint-Size."

Eyebrows slams him against a wall. "I'm so sick of your mouth."

"Well, unfortunately, your opinion doesn't sponsor me so I don't care what you're sick of."

"You have no idea the pleasure I would get to *accidentally* shoot you in the face right now."

Nulo smiles and says through his teeth, "Watch your mouth!"

"Or what, you're going to shoot me? Because I don't have to rely on an arm cannon to know that I'm good. Because I'm a real soldier, loyal to the Arvelee, and not an Iota puppet."

"Says the one holding the pointed AC."

Eyebrows quickly takes off his arm cannon. "That's it, let's go bare knuckles! Let's see if this mouth of Nulo's matches his big reputation."

Nulo chuckles at the two maphletes. "Are you guys about to jump me?"

"Naw." Eyebrows laughs. "I'm just gonna pound your face to a bloody pulp and announce to the ship how much of a fraud you really are." Eyebrows cackles at Nulo's shocked face. "You really think the ship likes you just because you have a bunch of sponsors?"

"That's more of a reason for you all to fear me."

"You think we're scared of the Iotas? By the time I'm done with you, you're going to be sponsored by the pharmacy." Nulo looks down the empty presidential halls and realizes there is no one to help in this oncoming battle. Eyebrows stretches his triceps. "You better have your resus cards ready, because that ankle will be the last of your worries."

"Do you always talk this much? Because it sounds like you're stalling."

Pint-size checks the time and dims the hall light. "Let's make this quick before we get in trouble."

"Too late." Nulo sucker punches Pint-Size just as he turns back. Nulo chops Eyebrows in the throat and strikes Pint-Size again, this time to the ground. Eyebrows returns with a dropkick to Nulo's hyper-extended leg. Nulo falls to one knee and curls to protect himself.

Eyebrows throws a combination of punches to all the soft spots of Nulo's body and says, "I should've known you had tricks up your sleeve."

Nulo counters the attack and desperately body slams him onto Pint-Size. Nulo stands over his aggressor and starts stomping Eyebrows. "You wanted to fight, come on."

From the ground, Pint-Size bites Nulo in his bad ankle and pulls him to the ground. He grabs Nulo's hair and smashes his nose against the floor. Nulo swings his arms to grab ahold of Pint-Size, but is caught by Eyebrow locking them from behind. "That tongue of yours isn't so sharp now, is it?"

The elevator door chimes and both maphletes straighten up, leaving an injured Nulo on his knees. Nulo spits out a wad of blood. "Ha, I thought you said you weren't going to jump me?"

The elevator dings and the doors open. Nulo sees Opha inside being escorted by his own set of maphletes. They shove Opha out of the elevator and he growls at the sight of Nulo on his knees. Nulo coughs and says, "Hey, O, listen, I'm going to take care of all this. I promise you."

Opha ignores him, walking quietly into his interrogation suite.

Nulo is picked up and thrown face first into the elevator. He struggles to his feet. "Good round, fellas, but you better lay low when I get my AC back."

Eyebrows steps into the elevator, grips Nulo's neck and whispers, "I'm not worried at all. Because once word gets out you don't have a working AC, everybody is going to want a piece of you."

"Like this." Pint-Size quickly punches Nulo in the ribs.

The elevator shakes as it descends many floors before stopping on the lobby level. The doors open for Dena, who is shocked and frightened by Nulo's appearance. She enters and stands on the opposite side of the three. She tries to ignore the obvious and casually whistles in the corner. Glancing quickly at Nulo, they make eye contact unintentionally.

Looking ashamed, Nulo shakes his head and tries to explain. "It's not what it looks like. These two idiots just jumped me."

Dena politely nods her head and watches Nulo's blood drip to the floor. Dena tilts her face in the other direction, but feels Nulo's eyes on her. She scoots closer towards the doors and directs her attention up at the glowing numbers as they decrease. Level B2 chimes and the maphletes hurl Nulo out of the elevator when the doors open. Nulo peers back at

Dena and blows her a kiss. An unresponsive Dena steps back and watches Nulo wave as the doors close.

.   .   .   .

She checks her TDA for further GPS instructions and proceeds to the presidential level as planned. Dena becomes nervous once the doors crack open. She stays in the elevator and whispers to herself, "This is dumb. What if Locy is right about everything?"

A security maphlete looks inside the elevator. "Are you coming out?" Dena nods and drags her feet as she exits.

The maphlete asks, "How can I help you, Commander?"

Dena glances over his shoulder and softly states, "Um, I'm here to speak with Admiral Arvelee or Captain Lyme, please."

The maphlete takes a second look inside the elevator. "Where's your escort, itinerary or packaged QP card?"

Dena stutters, "I don't ... have any of those things so wha- what can I do just to have a brief word with the captain? It will be really quick."

"Speaking with the admiral will never happen and to even board this level you need to barter over 100,000 quota points."

"Are you kidding me?"

"No, Commander, I am not and if you don't have any of the three, I suggest you exit this floor and come back more prepared at a later date."

Dena confidently scans her TDA under a sensor to transfer the 100,000 quota points. The sensor chimes to confirm the exchange and the maphlete steps aside to let her enter the floor. He points her towards the receptionist desk. When Dena is safely out of his sight, her tough demeanor immediately crumbles. "What did I just do? 100,000? You have just lost your life savings without thinking. Good job, Dena."

She looks over to see hundreds of chatting maphletes operating in cubicles and control panels. "So this is what Arvelee production looks like." Dena stops and stands in front of a heavily worked receptionist at a switchboard desk. She reads the name 'Fotaria' on the nameplate and blurts, "Excuse me, Fotaria?"

"Yes?" she answers.

"My name is Commander Dena from the lobby division and I'm looking to set up a meeting with Captain Lyme."

Without looking up, Fotaria rapidly states, "Is it upgrade matter, harassment, bartering issues, q-point errors, infections, or courtship that need to be addressed right away?"

"Wow, um, I just have a question about our life."

Fotaria cuts her off with an index finger to answer the switchboard. "Control, go ahead... thank you, connecting." She hangs up and tells Dena to continue.

Dena clears her throat. "Can I just ask Captain Lyme about – about, uh, some personal issues?"

Fotaria snickers. "Get in line, Commander. We all have issues. Your best bet is to write it down, drop it in the suggestion box and hope she'll respond. Please hold." Fotaria answers another call on the switchboard. Dena obediently grabs a pen a paper and turns away to hide her disappointment.

. . . .

"I hate this boat!" Sultri mumbles, "No, as a matter of fact, I hate my life." He inserts a few unmarked cards in his TDA while sitting in Grae's dark condominium.

Grae finishes counting his 90 q-points from Sultri and says, "Then leave."

"I wish it was that easy."

"But it is. All you need is an image and boarding card."

"Oh yeah, I'll just walk up to an Iota member and ask, 'excuse me, can I borrow a couple clearance cards so I can leave the Arvelee?' Yeah, that sounds like suicide to me."

Grae pulls out two rare memory cards. "No need to do something stupid like that when you can buy them off me."

Sultri is shocked at the sight of the colorful cards. "I never thought I'd see these cards in person. How do they work?"

Grae inserts the image card into his TDA and his symbolic birthmark changes color and shifts to another city ship's design. "See? The image card helps you blend in with foreign phages. The boarding card will get you on any ship without ever expiring."

Sultri has second thoughts and pushes the cards back. "I don't know about this. It just smells like trouble."

"Listen, you don't have the best reputation on board. What happened earlier was me being nice, again. Other card dealers would've handled you much *differently,* if you're getting what I'm saying. I think it's time for you to start over somewhere else."

"Then I will be running from some unfinished business. Defeated. I can't allow this ship to get away with all this unwarranted favoritism." Sultri starts to feel the adrenaline from the inserted cards and suddenly punches a back wall out of rage.

Grae ducks. "What are you doing? Are you trying to bring attention to my place?"

Sultri massages his scraped knuckles and sighs. "I just wish the Iotas would accept one meeting with me so I can explain to them what's happening. Because if we keep going down this worshipping route, we might as well name this city ship after Nulo."

They hear a soft knock on the door. Grae looks back at Sultri. "You see? You got these nosey neighbors knocking on my door now."

"I'm sorry," Sultri whispers while tiptoeing back to his seat.

Grae gathers up his scattered memory cards and shoves them underneath his sofa. He asks, "Did anyone follow you?"

"No." Sultri shrugs.

"Are you sure?"

"Positive."

Grae approaches the door with caution and opens it with the chain still attached. "Yeah?" A small pudgy woman appears and asks with urgency, "I hear you're the one with cards?"

"Nope." Grae tries to slam the door.

The mysterious phage stops the door with her foot and asks, "Well, do you know where I can find Ribonu?"

"Sorry, never heard of them." Grae shoves the door closed and locks it. Sultri hears the door slam. "What was that about?"

"I don't know, but she looked creepy."

"So you're judging potential clients by the way they look now?"

"Yes absolutely. That's how I stay open. She could've been an Iota spy or something." Grae enters his kitchen and Sultri secretly steals a QP card that fell on the ground.

71

Grae returns with a drink and asks, "Have you ever thought about going to see a maphlete about the favoritism?"

"I just did." Sultri grunts. "He told me something like 'work harder' and quit focusing on Nulo."

"Nulo is who you're complaining about? There is no comparison between you two. Nulo has always been blatantly honest, which gives him character. We know what to expect with him. And you can't even tell your own friend that you're short q-points."

Sultri slaps his forehead. "Not you, too?"

"It's the truth. If I had the respect he had around the Arvelee, no one would ever try to shortchange me. That's what I want."

"But you don't understand. All the lieutenants hate him."

"But all the ladies love him and I love the ladies. So he must be doing something right."

Sultri jumps up and kicks past Grae's legs. "Move."

"Where are you going?"

"To pay a visit to the captain. I told you my girlfriend, Fotaria, works up there as a receptionist and could probably set me up with a meeting."

Grae suggests, "Maybe you should wait until tomorrow, when you're cooled down and not speaking out of rage."

"I'm fine."

"But you're not. I just saw you insert three of those x5 cards and I'm pretty sure adrenaline is flowing all through your body now."

"It helps take the edge off. Now I can be honest when I'm speaking."

Grae laughs. "That's even more of a reason for you not to go. Those cards are gonna have you speaking faster than your thoughts can process."

"Listen." Sultri leans forward. "I don't listen to anyone who likes Nulo as a person." Sultri slides the QP card in his pocket and exits Grae's condo without looking back.

. . . .

Nulo stumbles inside his condominium and throws his deactivated arm cannon on the counter in disgust. Nulo flicks the light on to see his bachelor pad filled with clothes, empty cans and dirty dishes. He steps over a pile of clothes, grabs a beverage from the refrigerator and presses play on his answering messenger.

The machine beeps with the first message. "Hey, Nulo, I can't believe you pulled a stunt like that today, you never cease to amaze me. It's Dawit with LTE. Hope to see you on the next one."

Then the second. "Wow, you are crazy, man, craaaazy. I'm sorry, this is Bulpi, and I want to talk to you about partnership with the Iota DYT when you get a moment. You made me a lot of q-points today and I think this would be a good look for us both. Hope to talk to you soon."

Nulo smiles and says out loud, "You see? Those are fans; phages that appreciate the hard work I put in."

A third message plays. "I'm going to kill you. I almost got demoted because of you. I had to beg the council not to suspend me, but now I have a fine for 200 q-points in which you're going to pay. Not me. So call me back. This is Opha."

Nulo kicks through the trash and redials Opha from his room's TDA. As he waits for Opha to answer, he begins to reflect on his past trophies on the shelf. He reminisces as he looks at his many framed pictures, highlights and awards he has received from previous battles. In one of the pictures, he sees a younger Ghii, Esko and himself posing together. The newspaper headline reads, "Officers of the Quarter". He remembers a time where they were close friends and would encourage each other with chants:

"Me, Esko & Ghii! The Dynasty."

"The Three, Arvelee are we."

"Aye yoo, Aye yoooo."

"Hello?" Opha answers and repeats, "Hello."

Nulo snaps out of his daydream. "Hey listen, I - I really didn't mean to bring you in on all this. I really messed up this time, but I'm sure I can fix it."

"I'm mad at myself, mostly. I can expect these things from you, but agreeing to do it really upset me."

"You were behind on your numbers, remember? I was just being a friend."

"But you're not. You're a virus in disguise. If you don't change this selfish personality of yours, you will sink this ship before we know it."

Nulo is stunned, but replies carefully. "Alright, Opha, sounds like you're speaking out of anger. I've been in your position many times and trust me when I say, you have nothing to worry about."

"I'm done with you. Do you hear me? I'm done..."

Frustrated by the chain of events, Nulo zones out and hangs up. He yells, "This whole ship is ungrateful; even my so-called friends. If it wasn't for me, this ship would be dropping Nicil bombs on every shift."

Nulo limps into his bathroom and abruptly pushes his toiletries to the floor. He twists the sinks knobs and douses his face with handfuls of cold water. He looks up, wipes the blood from his face, and stares at himself in the mirror. "I can't be the problem, can I? I'm a good person doing what

I'm supposed to do." He pulls the mirrored door open to find something for his wounds and comes up empty.

"Did I use all my resuscitation cards?" He flicks and shoves gauze, hibiscus chargers and empty cards out of the way and slams the door shut. "Can my luck get any worse today?" He goes back to the living room, grabs his AC and proceeds to exit the condominium.

As he steps out into the hallway, he collides with a maphlete running past his door. Nulo drops his AC and shouts, "Watch where you going." The frightened female maphlete picks up and hands Nulo his AC before scurrying away. Nulo attaches it to his forearm and answers his previous question, "I guess it *can* get worse."

.   .   .   .

Grae finishes a transaction with a new set of customers and walks them to the exit. "Alright fellas, if you get caught with those image cards, you don't know me."

Grae looks in the other direction and sees his old girlfriend. "Nushaka."

Nushaka turns around and smiles when she sees him. "Hey, long time no see. Where have you been?"

"You know, here and there."

"Last I heard from you, you didn't pass the lieutenant's exam and just fell off the radar."

"I guess being a lieutenant wasn't for me."

"But you were so amazing at it. What happened?"

"Ah, I got better at other things." Grae pulls Nushaka inside his cabin and quietly reveals, "I sell cards now."

Nushaka's eyes widen. "Illegal cards?"

"Yeah. This is what everyone is working for right?"

"But this isn't you at all. You're one of the nicest phages I've ever meet and card dealers are ruthless and shady. Did you hear about Obatrius getting caught by the Iotas doing the same stupid thing?"

"I know, I know. The difference is Obatrius isn't as smart as I am. He sold to everyone *and* overpriced them. Listen, the pharmacies sells resus cards for thirty points and I sell them for twenty. And boarding cards are so exclusive I can easily get sixty points a pop. And if I sell three of those, I'm safe from the 1%."

Nushaka shakes her head. "Please don't play around with the Iota. They are really cracking down on anything out of the ordinary and I don't want you end up like Obatrius. You know they shut down my linguistics group because they said it was threatening?"

"Trust me, Nushaka, I'll be extra careful." Grae asks, "Are you still trying to save the planet and become this almighty maphlete?"

"Yup, any chance I can. Which reminds me, I'm starting a fighting league and I think you should join us. It's going to be fun and competitive. It's not confirmed, but I might have Nulo join us."

"Naw, that's okay."

"Why not? There is no future in selling cards."

Grae moves closer to Nushaka. "But what about our future? Do you see me in yours?"

Nushaka looks up into Grae's eyes and softly says, "I do ... but not like this."

"Trust me; selling cards is not as bad as everyone thinks it is. I'm smarter now and free to do whatever I want."

Nushaka stutters, "I – I have to go. I'm meeting up with some friends soon."

"Just tell me what I need to do to make things right with us." Nushaka speaks in a foreign language, "Be wise and try to better yourself. As long as you're selling those cards, we will never advance in life."

Nushaka bursts out of Grae's condo and leaves his door open.

Grae watches her strut off. "How in the world did I mess that one up?"

Suddenly his TDA vibrates a text message that reads, "Cul-de-sac in 30 minutes." Grae rushes behind the counter and fumbles inside his backpack. He counts what cards he has to offer and quickly leaves.

.   .   .   .

"Get your greasy hands off of me," yells Sultri, juiced from his x5 cards.

Dena looks up and sees the exiguous lieutenant causing a scene with the security maphlete at the elevator. The maphlete shoves Sultri back. "Answer the question, do you have an escort or not?"

Sultri slaps his hand away and yells, "I don't need an escort." He flashes the stolen gold QP card in the maphlete's face and forces himself inside. Dena keeps her head down, but secretly watches Sultri mumble and march up to the receptionist.

He slams his hands on the desk. "Fotaria, go get the Captain."

Fotaria is completely frozen from his unplanned arrival and stutters, "Sultri, wha- what are you doing up here? I'm working."

"I'll explain later. Just do what I said."

Fotaria leans over and whispers, "I'm going to take my break now so you and I can talk alone, okay?" As she reaches for her things, Sultri snatches her wrist. "No, I'm not waiting anymore. Call the captain out here now."

"Alright, just let go of me."

"Not until I get what I want! So start pushing buttons and get her out here now."

Fotaria tries to pull free from his grasp, but Sultri firmly sinks his nails into her frail arm. "Help!" she screams. "Someone get him off me."

Amidst the commotion, Captain Lyme anonymously appears through the crowd of bystanders. She doesn't introduce herself, seeing that her identity has always been a secret to the masses. Captain Lyme is a thin, petite woman with pale milky skin. She makes her way to the front and demands, "Do what she says."

After a few more tugs, Sultri finally lets Fotaria go. "And who is this, Fotaria, your bodyguard?"

Captain Lyme ignores Sultri and aids Fotaria's bruised wrist. "Are you okay?"

Fotaria weeps and shamefully answers, "I'll be fine."

The captain whispers something into Fotaria's ear and she calmly nods. Captain Lyme slowly escorts Fotaria to a back hallway and says, "Don't worry; you're excused from your shift."

"Fotaria," Sultri yells to his girlfriend. "We're not done talking. Get back here."

Fotaria scurries away, but the captain blocks Sultri. Still remaining anonymous, Captain Lyme quietly asks, "I can help you, sir. What seems to be the problem?"

"There isn't a problem. I was just talking to her." He shoves Captain Lyme out of the way and yells, "Fotaria get back here!"

She grabs his elbow before he can go too far. "Please lower your voice. I'm trying to help you."

Sultri raises it instead. "I'll lower my voice when I see Captain Lyme's face."

Captain Lyme signals security and Sultri sees the maphlete approaching. "What did I do wrong? I asked to see the captain and no one around here wants to help me."

The security maphlete asks, "Do you mind coming with me, sir?"

"Yes, I do." He looks at Captain Lyme and squints. "Why does everybody keep treating me like this?" Sultri tries to repress his rage and breathes forcibly through flared nostrils.

The security maphlete tries to grab Sultri's elbow. "Please sir, right this way."

"I said, no." Sultri pushes the security away. Sultri tightly balls his fists and cries, "I tried to be nice all day, but now I am done." He looks around and sees more maphletes closing in.

Dena and others are escorted out of the area and into the maphlete's cubicles. Dena stands on her toes, peeking over the top of the partitions to watch.

Sultri is surrounded and outnumbered by maphletes, all with loaded ACs. His teeth chatter and sweat beads across his brow. He remembers the x5 cards he injected earlier and cannot control the inundation of endorphins in his blood stream. Sultri's vision blurs, doubles and the surrounding voices start to echo. He closes his burning eyes and hears from a maphlete, "Come with us, sir."

Sultri opens his eyes and looks past the threatening maphlete. His heart rate increases. Sultri lets go of reason and allows his imprisoned rage to take over. He secretly activates his arm cannon. "The answer is still no!" Sultri head-butts the maphlete and elbows two others in the groin. He

80

reaches back and prepares to throw his strongest radiant fireball at the innocent woman's face.

"No!" Dena rushes forward to help, but is pulled back by concerned maphletes. She leaps over shoulders and pushes through to see Sultri staring at his open empty barrel; seconds before being tackled by maphletes.

The confident captain points to the exit. "Get him out of here, now."

They remove Sultri's arm cannon and check for other weapons. One of the maphletes finds the illegal memory cards stashed in his back pocket. The maphlete reports, "He's holding unmarked cards."

Sultri understands the repercussions and pleads, "Wait, wait. Those aren't mine." The captain asks, "Are you selling cards?"

"No, absolutely not. I bought them from a friend."

"A friend?"

"No, I mean he's just a guy I know."

"Who?"

Sultri uses his leverage and attempts to negotiate. "Will you go get the captain if I tell you his name?"

"Yes. You have my word."

Sultri thinks about his betrayal and closes his eyes momentarily. He expels a long breath and says, "They are from an officer named Grae."

Captain Lyme looks at a maphlete and gives the orders to locate Grae with a hand gesture. Sultri demands, "You got what you wanted now bring out the captain."

The grinning captain ignores his request and explains, "You are under arrest for attempted murder, possession and bribery. Anything you say or do will expedite your purging."

81

Lieutenant Sultri is furious as he is lifted to his feet. "I should've known I couldn't trust you and this scandalous ship. Who are you anyway?"

"Get him out of here."

"I curse this ship. I wish to see the day the Arvelee sinks."

One of the maphletes punches Sultri in the stomach and yells, "Shut up."

Dena's concern for the troubled lieutenant shows on her face. Sultri spots her through the crowd and says, "If I was you, I would find the quickest way to escape this floating prison. The whole operation is a set-up."

The maphletes drag Sultri's body through a side exit and Dena watches his fingertips grip the doorframe as he struggles to stay in the room. Just before he disappears he yells, "Get off the ship."

. . . .

Nulo limps through the Arvelee's active courtyard and enters the very popular promenade area. It's a cul-de-sac of various storefronts that curve in the nose of the ship. Each business is self-owned by phages that chose the business ultimatum instead of the soldier route. The courtyard's foot traffic never sleeps and has become the default meeting place of the Arvelee.

A sassy, strutting woman appears behind Nulo with a seductive fragrance that forces him to turn around. She quickly lets down her red, bouncy ponytail to purposely cover a name badge that reads "Kulinda". She flirts.

"Mmm, the infamous Nulo."

He squints and says, "Heeeey, um..."

"Don't worry big guy, we've never met." Kulinda reaches inside her blazer and offers him a deluxe QP memory card.

Nulo accepts it and asks, "What's this for?"

"It's 10,000 quota points for your hard work inside the mezzanine. My boss has been watching you for some time now and I must agree that I'm impressed."

Nulo now realizes she's an Iota sponsor. "Oh, thanks. And thank you so much for this. I definitely needed to hear that."

She smiles. "No problem. I can't wait to see you on the next one."

Nulo clears his throat. "Yeah, um, about that. I've kind of been demoted by some knucklehead maphlete and could use a favor to get me back in there."

Kulinda nods. "Consider it done."

"Wow, thank you." Nulo tries to hug Kulinda, but she quickly stiff-arms him in the chest.

"Slow down, big guy, a hand shake would work just as well." she explains.

"Okay." He awkwardly extends his hand. "And I didn't catch your name?"

"Because I didn't throw it." She firmly shakes his hand and walks away.

Nulo watches her strut through the crowd and shrugs. "That was embarrassing, but you gotta love the Iota's power."

He looks at the given memory card and deposits the 10,000 inside his TDA.

. . . .

Further inside the promenade, two young officers are being arrested by some maphletes. A crowd begins to form as they're escorted through the courtyard. "We didn't do anything," cries one of the officers.

The maphlete answers, "All I want to know is where's the 'cove' we keep hearing about?"

"Cove, what's that?"

"I'm done playing with these fools, now it's time to make them an example. Let's take them down to the propellers and get some real answers."

"No," the busted adolescents scream in unison, "not the propellers."

The maphletes don't waste any time and scoop the officers from the ground with their fire activated heel rockets. The two maphletes zip over the crowded promenade and pass over Grae during a transaction.

Grae follows the soaring maphletes above and quietly reiterates on his TDA, "No, I can't help you. I've done favors one too many times this week and I'm finally putting my foot down. I'm sorry, call me back when you have more." Grae disconnects and apologizes to another customer standing behind him. "Sorry about that. What type of cards were you looking for?"

Ironically, the customer turns out to be the crying Fotaria. She smears the makeup from under her eyes and says, "I need four resus and a boarding card."

"Alright." Grae secretly looks at her voluptuous figure as he digs inside his backpack. He recognizes her name as he reads her badge. Grae asks, "Fotaria? Hmm, do I know you from somewhere?"

"No."

"Were you an officer with me a few years ago?"

"No, I've been a receptionist for the past four years. Now can we move this transaction along a little faster, please?"

Grae finally connects her with Sultri. He finds the correct number of cards she requested, but feels uneasy about selling them to her. Grae tucks the cards back inside his bag and asks, "Are you forced to leave because of Sultri?"

84

Busted, Fotaria blinks rapidly. "What? How do you know him?"

"Sultri is a customer of mine and brought your name up earlier. I was kind of worried about him supped up on X5s as he stormed out."

Fotaria starts to cry louder. "He's so stupid."

"Why, what did he do up there?"

"It doesn't matter now. He's probably dead or getting tortured for answers. And that's why I gotta get as far away from this ship as possible."

Grae, filled with corrupted motives, gently holds her forearms. "I want to help and possibly leave the Arvelee with you."

"With me?" Fotaria exclaims. "I don't know you like that. You're just a shady card dealer probably looking to rob me blind."

"Shady?" Grae jokingly holds his chest and falls to the ground. He struggles to pull out a resuscitation card and inserts it inside his TDA.

Confused, Fotaria asks, "Are you okay?"

Grae exaggerates a fake heart attack and explains, "I am now. You just *really* hurt my feelings with that."

Fotaria reserves her smile and eventually laughs. "That was good. You actually fooled me."

"*And* scene. Thank you, thank you." Grae playfully drops into a curtsy.

"I'm starting to get the feeling that you flirt with all your customers."

"Not at all. Only the females." Fotaria laughs out loud and finally loosens up. "There's that beautiful smile I've been looking for."

Bashful, Fotaria sighs. "So, what's your name, Mr. Card Dealer?"

"Whoa, I don't know you," Grae mimics her voice. "You could be a shady Iota spy looking to screw me over."

Fotaria winks. "You never know."

Grae opens her hand and writes coordinates to his condominium. "If you're serious about leaving, meet me back at my place so I can pack the rest of my things. And that barter card will be on the house."

. . . .

Shaken by Sultri's arrest, Dena nervously taps her feet in a force of habit. Suddenly, Director Arooni steps off of the elevator with her face covered under her maphlete hood. The androgenic Arooni is respected, but also known to be the short-tempered voice of the captain. She quietly walks past Dena and approaches the switchboard desk. Arooni slowly removes her hood, revealing an exhausted edifice.

"This can't be good." Knowing Arooni's reputation, Dena looks towards the elevator and decides to abort her original plan.

At the doors, Captain Lyme her calls, "Commander!"

Dena hears her title, but fearfully ignores it. She rapidly presses the call button and hears the captain signal a maphlete. "Someone grab her before she leaves."

Dena is forced to turn around and sees the woman standing with an extended arm. Choking to swallow, she wonders what she has done. The captain removes her earpiece surveillance and hands it over to Arooni. She meets Dena and calmly states, "Come with me, please."

Dena feels the security maphlete nudging her to follow.

Captain Lyme leads her down a bright, narrow hallway and whistles a familiar tune to Dena. They enter a luxurious suite with the entire solar system painted in detail on all four walls. Dena ducks and maneuvers around scattered, draped stars suspended from the ceiling and follows the captain inside.

86

The captain offers her a seat at a table and Dena slowly accepts it. She asks, "Commander, you've been on the Arvelee for how long?"

"A little over ten years."

"And I hear you have questions concerning the Arvelee?"

Dena retreats from the conversation. "Yeah, but I'm patient. I don't want to burden you or anyone who has to make that happen. And if you're wondering, I had nothing to do with that crazy lieutenant. I don't know why he was specifically talking to me. I don't know him and have never seen him before in my life."

Captain Lyme doesn't respond, making Dena even more uncomfortable. Suddenly the sound of a boiling tea kettle pierces the silence and startles the already apprehensive commander. "Excuse me." The captain clears her throat and goes to prepare a cup of tea. She calmly removes the kettle from the heat and pours the boiling water inside a copper mug. "Would you like some tea?"

Dena takes a moment to answer. "No, thank you." Captain Lyme dips a packet inside the mug and takes a slow sip. Dena watches as the captain closes her eyes and inhales the aroma. She breaks the silence. "Did I do something wrong?"

The captain continues to hold the cup under her nose and answers, "Absolutely not."

"So why did you bring me in here?"

"Because you're looking for answers, right?"

Dena sighs. "Yes, but it's not that urgent."

"But it is. The prophecy told me you were coming, but I didn't think it would be this soon." Dena suspiciously looks around confused and quietly asks, "Captain Lyme?"

She smiles. "Yes, and it's wonderful to finally meet you."

CHAPTER 7

Lieutenant Nulo enters Sharlo's Diner, a tavern frequented by active lieutenants and commanders, and is greeted by fans and fellow soldiers. Nulo salutes the bar regulars and tickles Sharlo, who has her back turned.

"Psst," Nulo whispers.

Sharlo jumps and greets her good friend. "Hey there."

"How's your day been?"

"You know, the usual screaming and fighting, followed by threats. Then there's me asking myself why I'm still working here."

"Yeah that pretty much sums up my last couple hours."

"Oh yeah I heard there was a close call in the arena today. Are you okay?"

"Yeah I'll tell you about it. Could you cook me up the usual and I'll pay once I finish talking to the doc?"

"Sure, coming right up."

Nulo limps through the busy bar and travels through the kitchen. He enters a secret series of doors and obstacles and stops at a key-padded wall. He types in the four-digit code and proceeds inside the Arvelee's exclusive black market.

The Cove is a dark gritty room filled with candles in open jars mounted along the walls. It holds a mixture of smells and several aisles of stacked crates. Nulo locates his mentor, Dr. Ribonu. "Hey doc, you might want to change the passcode or relocate the Cove, because some youngsters just got busted right out front."

Ribonu slaps his forehead. "I told them not to take their cards out until they got back to their rooms."

"Can the cards be traced to you?"

"Do I look dumb to you? Of course not."

Nulo shrugs. "Alright, enough with my fake concern. I need another box of resus cards."

Dr. Ribonu turns to Nulo with disgust. "Another one? That's two in a week. Who's trying to kill you now?"

"Oh it's nothing like that. I got into it with some knuckleheads earlier and I sprained my ankle in the arena."

"Now tell me the real story, like how you got demoted for your carelessness."

Shocked, Nulo stutters, "How did you hear about that?"

"I'm Dr. Ribonu. I know every bit of gossip that travels this city ship." Ribonu hands Nulo a dozen resuscitation cards and accepts Nulo's q-points from his TDA.

Nulo quickly opens the box and inserts a few cards in his slots. Nulo asks, "So if you know all the gossip, why did you ask me?"

"Because I wanted to see if you were going to tell me the truth. Which you obviously didn't."

"I really did fight a couple of maphletes."

"Oh, I believe you. These days you're making more enemies than friends."

"So be it. I like my circle small. The only ones who understand me are the Iota sponsors and, in my eyes, that's more important. Look, I just got an extra 10,000 points just for being Nulo."

"But they're not your friends Nulo. They're using you for their entertainment. Can't you see the Iotas are marketing you as a 'successful soldier' so others will get inspired?"

"Ok what's wrong with that?"

"Let's be honest, you're not the best to work with on board because you're stubborn. But yet the Iotas pay you more than anybody else for your over-the-top foolishness. That translates and inspires other soldiers that this is how you act to become successful."

Nulo takes an awkward moment and scoffs. "I guess you have the answers and you're my real friend, huh? An old washed up soldier who sells illegal Iota cards for a living."

Offended, Ribonu quickly lashes out. "What do you want from us?"

"Just a little recognition from this ship. Like a tribute that shows I'm one of the greatest soldiers in this division. Or even probably the planet."

"Wow, you sound like you are running a campaign to be the next admiral."

"I don't see why not. I'm doing more work than the captain and admiral put together." Without warning, Dr. Ribonu loses his balance and gags. "*Choshek.*"

Nulo, caught off guard, walks over to the dizzy doctor. "You okay?"

Ribonu quickly peers around the Cove; in search of something particular. He pushes Nulo out of the way and dips underneath the counter. Ribonu holds his head and snaps out of his daze. "I just had a vision."

"Of what?"

Before he could answer, Officer Riti, who hides his identity under a hood, walks into the Cove unannounced. He arrogantly struts past Nulo and browses through the merchandise. Nulo cautiously watches his every move.

Riti holds his throat indicating he can't speak and hands Dr. Ribonu a list of items. Nulo stares at Riti from the side, trying to get a glimpse of his face while Dr. Ribonu grants his request. "Coming right up."

91

Ribonu notices Riti using an older TDA and asks, "Would you like to update your TDA?"

"I'll be fine," Riti whispers with a raspy voice.

While Dr. Ribonu bags up his items, Riti lifts his head towards Nulo and calmly looks back down. Ribonu confirms, "Blueprints of the Tamin, a Kepler map and one IFX image card all in the bag."

Riti nods. Ribonu tallies the total. "That will be 3400 q-points. Would you like any formunition or resus cards?" Riti declines and waves his TDA under a sensor to transfer the points. Riti loads his items into a duffle bag and heads out without looking back.

The door slams and Nulo says, "You see what I'm saying? No respect for who I am. Did you see how he strolled in here like he didn't recognize me?"

Dr. Ribonu rolls his eyes and walks away. "Well, this *is* a black market. Some of the scummiest soldiers walk in and out of here concealing their identity."

"I don't like it. The Cove is starting to become too populated. Don't forget who your first and only customer was back in the day."

Ribonu smirks. "So you want me to shut my Cove down because I'm getting more business?"

Nulo frowns. "If those same customers start to jeopardize my time, yes."

. . . .

From the reception desk, Director Arooni compares the Arvelee's schedule with real time and frowns. She sends a system-wide text to all required parties. "Be advised, we are ten minutes off schedule, but the next barter will properly take place in thirty."

92

She rolls her chair to another screen and sees a recent unreported Nicil bomb release. Arooni scrolls through recent activities and looks for possible errors. "So this bomb really *was* activated today." Arooni lifts her TDA. "Maphlete Paxo, do you read me?"

A brief moment of silence passes before Paxo blurts, "This is Paxo, go ahead."

"I need to see you at the receptionist desk as soon as possible. Thank you."

"Copy."

Arooni spins around in the chair and sees Maphlete Esko leaning on the counter. He uses a seductive voice and asks, "How are things holding up, sweetheart?"

Ignoring that, Arooni asks, "Do you know anything about the Nicil bomb that was dropped earlier?"

Esko shrugs and stutters, "I - I heard there was a drop, but I thought you knew about it."

"I didn't. Can you tell me who authorized this?"

"I don't know. If not Ghii or Paxo, maybe it was the Captain."

Arooni rubs her chin and nods. "Now I have to do an incident report. How am I supposed to explain this to the Iota when I don't even know what happened?"

Esko smiles. "I'm sure everything will be fine once you speak with the other maphletes." Esko stands over Arooni and watches her type on the computer. He secretly admires her, but feels handicapped due to his prosthetic leg. He works up the nerve anyway and boldly asks, "Let me take you out sometime?"

Arooni blinks and looks up. "Excuse me?"

"I'm about to go out and get a bite to eat and wanted to know if you would like to join me. I feel like a few years ago we got off on the wrong foot and I would like to make it up to you."

"That's very kind of you, but I have a lot of work to finish up."

"If not today, maybe next week or the week after?"

Arooni looks directly into Esko's eyes. "The truth is, even if I had a week of time, I still wouldn't want to be associated with a soldier like you. Now, if you will excuse me, I really have to finish this." Esko feels the sting of rejection and slowly walks towards the elevator, trying to hide his red face.

. . . .

Commander Dena is baffled by the fact she is sitting with the esoteric captain of the Arvelee. She thinks back on everything that has happened and asks, "If you're Captain Lyme, why would you put yourself in such danger?"

"Well, why not?"

"Because you almost died trying to help that lunatic. I thought captains were supposed to be hidden away with the admiral."

"And if only he would've been patient, he would've received my help."

"But he could've killed you. What if he'd had a knife or something?"

"So be it. If anything happens to me, that'll be my destiny. Everything works together for a much greater plan for our purpose."

"Why are you speaking in riddles?"

"It's to give you confirmation and to re-inform your direction. I can only say so much and not interfere with what's to come."

"But if you know my personality, you will know I can handle truth. So trust me."

"Trust is a word that is derived from the truth. When our subconscious taps into a prophecy of unwanted news, we unintentionally try to fix the outcome."

Dena sighs. "Okay, now what does *that* mean?"

"If I tell you that you are going to die at the end of your work shift, there's a good chance you will avoid working it. Am I right?"

Dena gulps. "If it's my destiny, I guess I will have to do it."

"Will you, honestly?"

Ashamed, Dena exhales. "I don't know."

"Our thoughts are much stronger than our actions and free will is set to strengthen the two."

"But if you give me a solid assignment, you'll have to trust I will follow your every command."

Captain Lyme smiles. "You have good intentions, Dena, but when tested, chances are you'll fail.

. . . .

Nulo looks behind Ribonu's counter and asks, "What new stuff you got hidden back there?"

Ribonu picks up an octagon-shaped memory card and says, "This is new, it's called O4X. It's like a survival card packed with glycerol synthesis, electrolytes, antioxidants and fluid replenishment."

"Wow," Nulo says sarcastically and shrugs. "I'm not going to lie to you. I have no idea what those things mean."

"Food and water. These cards provide nourishment for a week, without physically eating or drinking."

"Oh. Nice."

Ribonu opens another case from the shelf. "I got exclusive sound wave reflectors, morph, numbing, tactical defense and pogo cards; which those shady local dealers can't get ahold of." Nulo grabs a pogo card at looks at it intently. "Which Beverod ship do you get this stuff from?"

"If I told you I would be out of business, now wouldn't I?"

Nulo laughs. "You're probably right. Do you ever use this stuff yourself?"

"I don't have to, watch." Dr. Ribonu removes a bandage wrapped around one of his hands. Ribonu creates a formulated glow pulsating with fire from his bare palm.

"Woo!" Nulo shouts when he sees the ball switch from red to yellow and spark to the ceiling. "You can shoot formulas without an AC?"

Ribonu winks. "Something like that." He closes his hand to extinguish the spray of fire. He rewraps his palm and says, "And that's why they call me the doctor."

"Can you do that for me?"

"Yeah."

"Are you serious?"

"Of course not."

Nulo approaches Ribonu with praying hands. "Come on."

"No this ship can't afford for you to abuse this type of power."

"How long have we known each other? You know I could use that more than anybody. That would really put me over the top."

"The answer is still no."

Sharlo reaches Nulo on his TDA. "Lieutenant, your meal is ready at table twenty-nine.

He brings his TDA to his face and responds, "Thank you, Shar, I'll be out in a second."

Nulo switches arms and lifts his arm cannon. "You see this useless thing? I can't do anything until it gets reactivated."

"Sorry."

"Well, can you at least rig my AC so I can still shoot?"

"You can't override a deactivated AC. As soon as it gets tampered with, it sends a signal to the maphletes and they'll shut it down."

"Sell me a new one?"

Ribonu folds his arms across his chest. "I can't, because you're my friend and I don't want to see you get in more trouble."

Nulo grabs his box of resus cards. "I'm not your friend, I'm a customer. Remember that." He stomps out of the Cove and heads back to the tavern.

. . . .

Captain Lyme continues to vaguely answer Dena's questions. "Even though I have the gift of premonition, I still can't control your intentions, only the initial outcome of your free will."

Dena begs, "At least tell me what's going on with the Iotas on the Beverod. Why are they forcing us to take these vaccine pills when we haven't had one reported case of Variablitus?"

Captain Lyme takes a sip of her tea and passively shrugs, leaving Dena in the dark.

Dena repeats, "Come on, Captain, you can give me *that* at least."

97

"Find the Aberash and you'll get *all* your answers."

"The what?"

"The Aberash. It'll lead you to the truth; it's the power of our purpose."

"Really now?" Dena sighs. "Why this is the first time I'm hearing of this word? Sounds like another riddle, Captain. Try again."

Captain Lyme walks around the table and rests her palm on Dena's chest and says, "You're heart is finally in sync with your purpose and needs you to let go."

"Please stop with these brain puzzles."

"Listen," the captain demands. "I've already broken the Treaty and said too much. And because of this, spies of the Iotas will notify the Beverod. So just do what I said and seek the Aberash."

"I don't mean to be rude, Captain, but my entire life has been following Arvelee laws. I finally meet you and you're telling me to forget everything and now *seek the Aberash*."

"I know it's confusing, but yes. "

"No, Captain, this is my life we're talking about. If this Aberash is so important, why hasn't it ever been mentioned in our laws? There are too many secrets around here, which makes it hard for me to trust what you are saying. Goodbye."

Captain Lyme stops Dena from leaving by softly saying, "Locy knows. She has felt it and she's not crazy."

"You know about Locy?" Dena desperately approaches the captain.

"Of course I do."

"Okay, but that still doesn't answer my question. Why haven't we heard about the Aberash?"

"You still don't get it." Captain Lyme calmly explains, "You've had the answers all along, you just have to dig deeper. Believing you have the answers is the first step."

Captain Lyme offers a handkerchief to catch a tear falling from Dena's face.

Dena lightly dries her cheek and tucks it inside her belt. Captain Lyme kisses Dena on the forehead and says, "Be on the lookout for a brave soldier with secrets of his own. Don't be so judgmental, because he'll be a stepping stone."

Dena smiles. "Yeah, I ran into him earlier."

Captain Lyme holds her temple and says, "How is that possible?"

"The guy you are referring to is Riti from Ship Amyn, right?"

Captain swiftly types in the city ship Amyn. A warning window flashes across the screen. "No Records." Captain Lyme quickly exits the room, running toward the front switchboard to Arooni.

Dena jogs close behind the captain. "Wait, Riti wasn't the soldier you were talking about?"

Captain Lyme ignores the question and rushes Arooni out of the seat. "Will you excuse me, Director? I need to locate a certain soldier from this computer."

Arooni obediently pops up from the chair and stands beside Dena.

Captain Lyme plops into the swivel chair and begins to frantically type.

Dena grabs her head. "Can someone please tell me what's going on?"

Arooni watches Captain Lyme type in coded information. "It appears you allowed a stowaway on board this ship."

"Technically, I didn't allow it. I questioned him and he didn't appear as a threat."

"Did you notify one of our maphletes so he could be analyzed, or quarantined?"

"No, because I..."

Arooni cuts her off. "Well you've put us all at risk because there isn't any record of anOfficer Riti from Amyn."

Arooni uses her shoulder to nudge Dena as she rushes away. She calls back, "Don't worry, Captain. I'm already on the search."

CHAPTER 8

Lieutenant Nushaka spots Nulo eating alone in the diner and approaches him. She snickers. "Hey there, it's me again."

Nulo squints and asks, "I'm sorry, who are you again?"

"Nushaka. You bumped into me earlier after our shift. I was telling you about the lieutenant league we were starting and wanted to know if you were interested."

"Mmm, that's right." He swallows his food and asks, "Have you found an elite representative to fund the league yet?"

"No, we're just starting with hopes we could use a few of your sponsorships to help us out."

He immediately loses interest. "Listen, you have a really good idea, but I know I wouldn't be any help to you with my crazy schedule. My sponsors are just as bad. Sorry."

"Oh, no problem. Thanks for the chat." Nushaka turns and shakes her head in exasperation towards a table full of friends.

Nulo takes another bite of his sandwich and wipes his mouth with the back of his wrist. He looks over to Nushaka's table and sees her friends giving him dirty looks. He says under his breath, "I'm so sorry I couldn't financially entertain you, but I was busy keeping this ship above water."

The headline from the evening news captures the attention of a passing lieutenant and he yells, "Hey, turn that up." Sharlo grabs the remote and increases the volume.

Nulo hears the reporter emphasize how expensive the recent mezzanine damages are and ducks deeper into his seat.

The bar shamefully frowns at the aftermath and sighs at Nulo's photo appearing across the screen.

Nulo hears sarcastic praise over the crowd's gurgling. "Let's give a round of applause to the heroic, super soldier eating alone over there."

The soldiers join the drunken Lieutenant Kaphir standing in ovation and laughing. Humiliated, Nulo preps to escape the surrounded mockery and exits his booth. He pays for his half-eaten meal and maneuvers through the insensitive crowd.

Kaphir quiets the crowd and stops Nulo at the doorway. "Aww, we were just having a little fun. Where are you running off to?"

With drowsy eyes, Nulo responds, "I had a long day and I just want to head to my condo and get some sleep."

"And you know what I want?" Kaphir asks. "An honest apology."

Nulo now recognizes Kaphir's face. "Come on, now. Are you really that petty?" Kaphir's extended silence gives Nulo his answer. Nulo bursts with frustration. "Fine, I'm sorry. I am so sorry for accidentally shooting you earlier."

The stubborn Kaphir sucks his teeth and doesn't accept his repentance. "Maybe I'd believe it more if you were on your knees."

Nulo scoffs. "That's not going to happen."

"I think it will."

Kaphir's crew begins to surround Nulo. He's outnumbered and carefully says, "Let's not do this, guys. I really don't want any trouble."

Kaphir laughs hysterically. "Who said we wanted trouble? I just want a real apology; one we all can believe. Now kneel."

Nulo looks over to Sharlo behind the bar and she agrees with a light nod. Nulo contemplates an exit strategy and looks around for options.

"Time is wasting, Nulo."

Before he can devise a plan, Nulo is kicked in the chest by the impatient Kaphir. Nulo stumbles back, but gets tossed forward by one of Kaphir's cronies. Nulo propels through the glass entrance and slides outside of the bar. Kaphir steps through the broken doorway and walks over the shattered pieces of glass. Nulo attempts to stand, but gets kicked back down.

"Here lies the infamous, Nulo," Kaphir says while standing over him. He grabs Nulo's head and pushes his face into the pebbles of glass. He asks, "How does it feel? Punished and powerless just like that? It hurts, doesn't it? I don't care what this ship believes. You're just another weak phage in my eyes. So the next time you feel the need to prance around here like you're untouchable, I want you to remember my face and this moment."

Nulo struggles and feels around for something to grab. As Kaphir stands up, laughing, he is blasted in the jaw by a brick. Kaphir falls to one knee, but bounces back invigorated.

"Woo, cheap shot from the super soldier. I should've known it that wasn't easy to take you down. Let's dance."

Kaphir licks his bloody lip and fires up his arm cannon. Nulo pushes off the ground, but stays low. The pedestrians in the courtyard start to scatter. Nulo puts some distance between himself and Kaphir, hiding behind the crossing foot traffic and says, "We're even."

Kaphir pitches two shots from his AC. Nulo tucks and rolls behind a trashcan and looks for something to use as a weapon. Kaphir shuffles to get a better shot and watches Nulo creep back toward the entrance of Sharlo's diner.

103

"There you are." Kaphir opens fire and Nulo uses others as a shield. Kaphir loses sight of him and yells, "Move. Everyone get down."

Nulo dives through the window and scrambles to take cover behind an overturned table. Sharlo tries to diffuse the situation. "Alright Kaphir, I think you've scared him enough."

Kaphir snaps, "No, I haven't."

"You are ripping my place apart, stop this."

"Put it on my tab. Shut up and let me do everybody a favor."

The smoke starts to clear inside the diner and Kaphir sees Nulo hiding behind the bar in the reflection of the ceiling's mirror. Kaphir playfully taunts Nulo as he inches towards him. "Come out, come out, wherever you are, super soldier."

Kaphir throws a stool behind the bar to force Nulo out in the open. Nulo flinches, but doesn't disperse. He starts to panic from his lack of options and yells, "Don't you think this has gone too far? Look at the damage you've done."

Kaphir climbs over a chair. "I don't know what you're talking about."

"You're going to shoot me with all these witnesses around?"

Nulo pops up from behind the bar with his hands raised. Kaphir whips up his AC and Nulo yells, "Wait! Think about what you are doing. Don't forget we are on the same side and should only be fighting Variables. What would the Iota do to you if they found about my death?"

Kaphir thinks about the extreme consequences and looks back at his nodding crew. He lowers his aimed arm and discreetly increases the power on his AC. Kaphir quickly spins back toward Nulo.

Someone fires out of nowhere. Kaphir slams into a booth, shattering a table in front of Nulo. Kaphir's back sizzles as he falls unconscious. Nulo looks up to see the shot came from Maphlete Ghii who is stepping through the pane of the shattered entrance. "No matter what punishment we hand you, we can't keep you out of trouble, huh?"

Nulo yells in defense, "Come on, you can't possibly think I started this."

Esko enters with a look of shame on his face. He shakes his head at the damages and tends to the palsied Kaphir.

Ghii points outside. "Witnesses said you struck him first."

"No, Ghii. He kicked me through the front door."

"*Maphlete* Ghii. Respect my title."

"Yeah, well take a number, Ghii, because that's something we are all looking to get around here."

Ghii grabs hold of Nulo's collar. "You're gonna learn sooner or later that Esko and I are your only allies. So at least act like we were once were friends."

Nulo smacks Ghii's hand away and shouts, "What do you guys want from me?"

"Cooperation. Tell us the truth so we can help you."

"I told you two what happened and I don't need to repeat myself. But if you want to know the truth, ask the owner, Sharlo. I'll be in my condo waiting for your apology." Nulo walks away, punches the wall and shakes loose glass from the frame as he exits.

. . . .

Dena wipes her tears. "I'm sorry, Captain. I never meant to put the ship in danger like that. He just told me he passes through."

Captain Lyme slaps the screen. "Found it!"

Dena leans over to look at the monitor and sees a profile of the ship Amyn with their Admiral. "What? Did you find Riti?"

"No, but I found his ship."

"Why did you say that name was unregistered?"

"Unregistered means we've never bartered with the Amyn. That city ship is in Division 11, six divisions away. Your friend has been travelling for quite some time now."

"I will accept whatever punishment you have for me."

"There's no punishment, Commander, because your purpose hasn't begun. Your curiosity made that bold decision, a choice that brought you here."

Dena exhales, relieved. "What now?"

Captain Lyme winks and walks away without answering.

Dena pulls out the folded handkerchief to wipe her nose and surprisingly finds a sparkling blue memory card buried inside. Underneath the card she finds a written message. *"Convincing one stubborn mind will soon convince thee and discover the power of the Aberash."* Dena is more confused than ever, but accepts the prophecy. She looks up to see her augural captain has vanished inside the crossing traffic of maphletes.

. . . .

Grae tidies his room and prepares for Fotaria's arrival. Embarrassed, he slouches at the sight of his trifling condominium while spraying a heavy load of air freshener. "I have to do better with my living situation."

Knock, Knock, Knock.

Grae pushes a stack of clutter off the kitchen counter and sweeps it under the couch. "That's about as good as it's gonna get."

106

Grae clears his throat and approaches the door with a confident strut. He looks through the peephole, but doesn't see anyone. "Who's out there?" Grae cautiously opens the door with the chain still attached.

The petite Locy surprises him through the crack of his door. "Are you Grae?"

"Who wants to know?"

Locy whispers, "Hey, if you're think I'm a maphlete, I'm not. I was told you were trustworthy and probably can get a hold of some cards for me."

"Nope, don't know what you are talking about. Sorry." Grae tries to push the door closed and Locy counters by leaning her weight against it.

"Grae, listen!" Locy explains. "You have to believe me when I say this ship is in danger and I really could use your help. Everyone knows you sell cards, okay? I was just saying that to make you feel like you're doing a great job at 'staying off the radar'. Now can you help me out or not?"

Grae shrugs. "What do you want?"

Locy sighs. "Thank you. I need to buy a boarding and image card from you."

Grae stoically looks down the hall and evaluates her motive.

Locy begs, "Trust me; this is not some sort of a sting to arrest you."

Grae reaches in his back pocket and holds out two cards. "If this concerns the life of our ship, these cards are on the house."

"Thank you." Locy graciously accepts them. "I promise you won't regret this." She darts down the hallway and quickly inserts the cards. She slowly feels some sort of side effect and suddenly becomes lightheaded. "What did he give me?" Locy falls to one knee and sees a scrabbled flash of orange appear. Her ghostly voices return very faint and tapers to silence.

Locy ejects both of the cards from her TDA and shockingly reads 'Iota vaccine' on the label. She can literally feel her heart stop. "Nooo!"

Locy stumbles back to Grae's door and screams, "You idiot. Do you realize what you just did?" She boldly kicks the door while trying to keep her balance.

Grae cracks it again with the chain attached and yells, "Get away from my door, you snitch, before you wake up the whole floor."

"Not until you give me what I want!"

Grae splashes ice water in her face causing her to choke mid-sentence.

Locy says, "You are as good as dead. And now we all are."

Safely behind his door, Grae mocks her. "Thanks for stopping by."

Grae watches her through the peephole and laughs at her when she eventually storms off. He returns to straighten up his place before Fotaria arrives.

Suddenly, there's another bold knock at the door. Grae scoffs. "Wow she is really getting on my nerves."

Before Grae could answer, he hears a masculine voice announce, "Officer Grae! We have a search warrant and we know you're in there. Open this door now."

Grae quietly leans in the peephole and sees two arresting maphletes. He whispers, "I knew that girl was a set-up." He ignores their demands and quickly retreats from the door. Grae starts to pack all incriminating cards into a bag and runs to his bedroom.

The maphlete repeats, "We're giving you until the count of three and we're coming in by force. One, two, three!" The Maphletes kick in Grae's door and rush inside with drawn arm cannons. "Find him!"

They trash every corner of Grae's condominium. They burst inside the master bedroom to find an open window and no Grae.

. . . .

Shortly after, Director Arooni urgently returns to the desk and asks a maphlete, "Where did the captain go?" The maphlete points to the back corridor and Arooni sprints down the hallway. Arooni turns a few corners and sees Captain Lyme entering a secured suite. "Captain, wait," Arooni yells.

Captain Lyme holds the door open and waits for her to catch up.

"I need to keep you up to speed," Arooni says. "I have a few maphletes searching for our latest intruder and there's another urgent issue that needs your attention."

Captain Lyme rests her palm over Arooni's collar and says, "It's time for you to lead this ship alone. Whatever you decide, you have my support."

"But I really think you should take a look at these gauge numbers and vitals."

"No, I need the rest more." Captain Lyme enters the room and shuts the door without another word. She drags her heavy feet to the center of the room and drops into a lotus pose to mediate.

After spending countless hours mediating in her sacred suite, Captain Lyme gasps when she is able to make a spiritual connection with Riti. She comforts him through telepathy. "I see all and I see you here. Don't be weary. The Aberash will guide you to your purpose."

CHAPTER 9

The radiant sun rises from behind the clouds and softly paints the warm skies orange. The Arvelee travels to the southernmost point of Division 5 where they are greeted by warm tropical weather.

Nulo's alarm unwelcomely repeats, *Your shift awaits*. He yawns and cringes from his sore jaw. Nulo kicks the alarm's speaker and covers his head with his pillow. He grunts hateful profanity and turns his back to the sunrise.

Bold footsteps parade through the hallway, stops and hovers in front of his condominium door. Nulo eyes flash open. He tilts his head and hears soft clicking inside the keyhole. Nulo quietly slithers out of his bed and reaches for his arm cannon on the counter. The door shatters open before he can reach it and he meets an enormous, mutated two-headed Variable storming in on all fours. The drooling, cross-eyed Variable claws its talons into the carpet and mirrors Nulo's every move. It leaps forward and choke slams Nulo against the wall, knocking his awards and trophies off the shelf. Crying, squirming, gasping for air, Nulo pounds the Variable's firm forearm desperate to weaken the grip. The beast leans into Nulo and slowly whispers, "We've found you and it's time to come with us."

"Never." Nulo closes his eyes tightly and feels the beast's breath roasting his cheek. He slips loose, falls, but slams into an enormous alarm clock. Your shift awaits, your shift awaits.

He yells as he wakes from the recurring nightmare. He doubles over from embarrassment and rubs the tears from his eyes. "It felt so real that time," he says as he unplugs his alarm clock and throws it against a wall.

Nulo jumps when he hears a knock on the door. "What now?"

Nulo tiptoes out of his room. "Who is it?"

"It's me. Open up."

"Anybody can say 'it's me'. What is your name?"

"Lieutenant Nushaka. I spoke to you yesterday in Sharlo's."

Nulo opens the door with the chain still attached. She is waving through the small crack.

"I already told you my answer and that's final."

"It's not that. I just need your advice."

He unhooks the chain and walks away without inviting her inside. He leans against the kitchen counter and folds his arms across his chest. "What is it?"

Nushaka follows him inside. "First of all, I'm sorry about what happened to you yesterday. That idiot was just causing trouble."

"Mmm hmm, is that it?"

"No." Nushaka reaches in her back pocket and hands Nulo a memory card. "I'm signing up for the future commander program and wanted to know if you would be my recommendation. You probably haven't seen me in action, so I put together sort of a highlight reel. I even added the time when a bunch of us took down that Leviathan in the 6th Aquarius season."

Without emotion, Nulo takes the card and mumbles, "I'll see what I can do."

"Oh, one more thing." She pulls out a sealed envelope and whispers, "This is a little embarrassing, but can you give this to your old friend Ghii for me? I kind of have a crush on him."

"Why would you think he's a friend of mine?"

"Everyone knows the history you, Esko and Ghii have. You guys were incredible together."

Nulo snatches it from Nushaka's hand with no real intentions of helping. "Sure. Now can you leave so I can start my miserable morning?" Nulo shoves her back into the hallway and slams the door shut. He throws her memory card onto a pile of other cards and stuffs the letter in his back pocket.

Looking in his bathroom mirror, he shakes his head. "Now they look at me as the ship's mail boy. Yup, my nightmares are becoming my reality." He skips the hygienic necessities and opts to mope around with the same filthy clothes from yesterday. He tucks his unregistered AC underneath his arm and cracks open a bottle of elixir for breakfast.

Nulo flinches as he relives a quick haunting scene from his nightmare. He tosses back the remaining liquid and welcomes the sting of the beverage as it travels down his throat. Nulo scratches his scruffy beard, throws the empty bottle on the counter and stares at the door. "Get it together. This demotion is just temporary." He slaps his cheeks and swings open the door. He sighs. "Here we go."

Nulo covers his face with the collar of his shawl to avoid running into any more situations. Detouring from his usual route, he takes the starboard stairs five flights above his destination. As he approaches the stairs, he hears Nushaka yell, "Wait a second."

Nulo ignores her and power walks ahead. She catches up and grabs Nulo before he reaches the exit. "I don't know what I was thinking, but that was really silly of me to give you that letter. Could I get that back so I can give it to Ghii myself?"

Nulo boldly lies, "Sorry, but I left it back in my room and I got to go."

"But your room is right there. Just run in and grab it for me."

"Listen, Lieutenant, I don't have time to entertain your secret love life of that bearded backstabber. I really have to go."

They hear screaming from down the hall. "Hey, hey Nulo!" It turns out to be Opha jogging in their direction.

Flustered, Nushaka begs Nulo, "Just promise me you won't tell anybody about the letter."

"I don't make promises; now move out of my way."

Opha arrives and interrupts. "I'm sorry, miss, but I really need to speak with my friend. Why have you been ducking my calls, you jerk?"

"I just got really busy and had to finish some stuff, alright?" Nulo tries to create a diversion. "Hey, Opha, have you ever met this fellow lieutenant of ours? Opha, Nushaka. Nushaka, Opha."

"I can't say that I have. Hi, how are you doing, Nushaka?"

As they are shaking hands, Nulo tries to tiptoe around, but is stopped by Opha's arm. "Hold on. Where are the 200 q-points you promised me?"

"In my room, I'll give them to you later."

Nulo bumps past their shoulders to leave and as he's walking away, he hears, "Well, well, well. Look who we have here." Lieutenant Kaphir claps his hands as he walks up behind Opha, his ruffian crew trailing behind. Kaphir rubs the cheek where Nulo struck him. "We have unfinished business, super soldier. I'm here for revenge. It sucks for you that those maphletes aren't going to protect you this time."

Nulo turns to Opha. "Thanks for being the cause of my death this morning, buddy."

Opha whispers, "What's going on?"

114

Nulo grabs Nushaka's shoulders and launches her into Kaphir as a diversion, before sprinting towards the exit.

Kaphir calls out, "Running just makes it worse. I'm a hunter and it is prey day."

Nulo frantically bursts through the double doors, ducking his head from shots fired. He turns and runs blindly down the murky flight of stairs, still dodging the wild gunfire. Leaping, he knows his life is riding on luck. He uses the flimsy banisters to tether his turns down the levels.

Kaphir's crew splits up in several directions to ensure Nulo's capture. Kaphir follows close behind and gallops down the stairs three at a time. His menacing voice echoes down and teases Nulo in the staircase. "I just want to talk, super soldier. I promise this time."

In that very instant, Nulo trips and falls over a wet floor sign between levels. Nulo crawls to a nearby mop bucket and flips the dingy water onto the floor. He throws the bucket down the flight of stairs as a distraction and hides in a custodian closet. While inside the cramped storage area, he forcibly slows down his breathing to stay quiet. He waits patiently, hoping his nemesis is duped by the wet floor.

Kaphir sees the mess and decreases his speed, carefully making his way through the wetness. Nulo holds his breath as he watches Kaphir's silhouette scroll pass the translucent window outside the door. He closes his eyes, confident his pounding heart is luring Kaphir towards the drab closet.

Kaphir stops in front of the door and Nulo sees the knob crank counter clockwise. He gently grabs the knob and prepares to tug the door. A distant voice yells, "I think he's down here."

Kaphir releases the knob and bolts away from the closet. Nulo exhales with relief and tries to regain his poise. He peeks his head through the door and sees another henchmen passing. Before he can yell out, Nulo chops him across the neck. The goon points his AC and Nulo catches it and cracks the glove against the wall before he shoots.

Nulo strikes him in the throat once again and continues to dismantle the AC against the wall. Nulo twists and flips him down on the damp floor in a chokehold. The hoodlum squirms and struggles in Nulo's hold as the oxygen slowly leaves his pale face. His body drops into slumber and Nulo finally releases his grip.

He cautiously gets to his feet and drags the unconscious body inside the custodian's closet. "I'm sorry, my friend, but this is what happens to Kaphir's followers." As Nulo stuffs the body inside the closet, a blinking cube catches his attention from beneath the staircase. Nulo locks the door and dashes below to analyze the object. He hears distant footsteps approaching, forcing him to leave it and run in the opposite direction.

.   .   .   .

Locy playfully knocks on Dena's condominium and notices her door is slightly open. She pushes it further open to discover her friend's place has been ransacked.

"Oh no!" Locy blurts. "The Iota got her. Dena!"

"Hey!" Dena pops up smiling from behind her couch, welcoming Locy inside.

Confused, Locy asks, "Uh, were you robbed? If so, you are taking this very well."

Dena ignores her question. "I think I figured out why you were having those visions and hearing those voices. I've done extensive research and it may be tied to our purpose."

Locy sighs. "I told you not to get involved in this. You were absolutely right, it was Variablitus. I was just too stubborn to admit it. Ironically, some idiot drugged me with vaccine cards and now the visions are gone."

"But you were right." Dena pulls out the handkerchief. "Look, this is from Captain Lyme. She told me we would need each other."

"Wait." Locy rejects the handkerchief. "You're socializing with the captain now? How?"

"I used 100,000 q points I saved up over the years."

"What?" Locy checks Dena's TDA. "You can't be serious. Did you really waste that many points for a captain chat?"

"Yes and it was all worth it. She knew everything about us. That meeting was divine. And now it's time for us to find this Aberash and see where that path leads us."

"Well, I didn't get that memo."

Dena pulls the vaccine pills out and asks, "Don't you want to at least know the real reason why the Beverod implemented these pills in all the ships?"

Stubbornly, Locy answers, "I just told you. It was to prevent us from getting Variablitus; the visions, the voices?"

Dena opens the handkerchief. "Listen, it says, *the battle to convince one to soon convince thee to discover the Aberash*. That's us, Locy. You made me aware of all this and now I have to convince you. What are you afraid of?"

"Of dying. I'm not trying to lose my life over some silly pills."

Dena unfolds her arms. "I guess I'll have to travel alone to the Beverod to get answers for the both of us."

"The Beverod?" Locy blurts. "You think you can just board the most sacred city ship on the planet with no repercussions? And *you* have the nerve to call *me* crazy."

"This was a prophetic word for the both of us. We have to honor it."

"You know how I know it wasn't prophetic? Because we have a shift that's starting and no replacements. Now let's get ready and stop talking this nonsense."

"I'm not going back in there, Locy. I can't go another day wondering if I could've made a difference in the world and didn't. That tiny thought would kill me if I returned to work ignoring what I just discovered."

Locy threatens Dena. "So you're telling me that our captain, Captain Lyme, told you we're supposed to skip our shift, which is a crime; leave our city ship, which is forbidden and travel to the Beverod, which is completely unheard of; to find something called the Aberash?"

"Yes."

Locy chuckles. "I want you to really think about what you are agreeing to. Once you realize it's a suicide mission, I'll be waiting for you at our post." She slowly exits Dena's condo, disgusted and mumbling to herself.

. . . .

Grae looks over his shoulder and darts through a basement hallway. He mumbles, "I guess it's time to take my own advice and leave the Arvelee." He hides in a corner and pulls out a boarding card and installs it. He stares at his bag and contemplates what to do with the rest of his cards. "This is a lot of points I'm missing out on and I certainly could use it while I'm gone." Grae gets an idea and bolts further down the hallway.

He heads to the bartering corridor and enters a rowdy room of young escorts. He looks at the front of the class and sees Officer Rhoddy begging, "No, no, no! Sultri's not here and I told you everything I know."

Grae quickly quiets Rhoddy down and pulls him to the side. "Listen, I'm not here to hurt you."

"Yeah, I heard that one before."

"This has nothing to do with you or Sultri, but I need a huge favor."

After chatting with Rhoddy, Grae announces to the class, "Listen up, escorts, my buddy here is allowing me to offer you a deal of a lifetime. Some of you I've worked with before, so you know I'm legit. I'm selling all of my cards half off. Everything must go."

Grae's previous customers confirm his credibility to others and quickly gather around him.

"Make this quick," Rhoddy begs. "And I want that AC5 like you promised."

"No problem Rhoddy." Grae maneuvers to the center of the room holding his back pack in the air. "One at a time. Everyone will get something, trust me." The escorts form a jagged line around the room while Grae starts his sells. He exchanges his cards with their q-points by locking their TDAs with one another.

The defeated Nulo peeks inside the classroom window. He double checks the number on the door to confirm. "Just my luck. A class full of floozies." Nulo walks in and slams the door shut to demand silence. The escorts scatter and Grae shoves his bag of cards underneath a desk.

Rhoddy meets Nulo at the door. "Oh, hey, Lieutenant Nulo! What brings you down to the bartering corridors?"

Nulo ignores his kind welcoming and asks, "Are you Rhoddy?"

"I sure am. How can I help you?"

"You're excused for the day and don't ask me why. Go home."

Flabbergasted, Rhoddy gathers his things and swiftly exits the room.

"Oh, no," Grae whispers. "They sent Nulo looking for me?" He ducks his head and hides in the crowd.

Without enthusiasm, Nulo says, "Alright, gather around. I have an announcement to make." The excited escorts circle Nulo, but get too close. "Hey, I don't like to be touched. Back up! My name is blah-blah-blah from the Who-Cares level. I will be your trainer for a couple of weeks, but that doesn't mean you have the right to ask me any questions. Now, do any of you have a question?"

Grae sees a few escorts stealing from his bag of cards and yells, "Hey!"

The crowd opens up and Grae is left in the center of the room.

Nulo sighs. "What's your question?"

Improvising, Grae asks, "Uh yeah, is it true that you once roughed up an Iota member for trying to cut a bad deal with you?"

Nulo laughs. "Uh, not exactly, but how'd you hear about that?"

Grae tries to tame his excitement and laughs. "Are you kidding me, who on this ship hasn't heard about 'Thee incomparable Lieutenant Nulo'?"

Nulo accepts the compliment and hears another officer add to the list of his achievements. "Yeah I heard you once took out over 200 Variables with only one formunition card. It's like you're not even trying."

The other escorts chime in with their most memorable moments of his battles.

Nulo's grin slowly turns into an embarrassing laugh as he takes a sudden trip down memory lane. He finally raises his arms and says, "Alright, alright, you guys, quiet down. Stop it, you're making me blush."

Grae steps forward. "In all honesty, sir, the respect you have on board is what I've always dreamed of."

I'm glad I inspire you," Nulo says with gratitude. "But why dream it when you can start to live it?" Grae shakes Nulo's hand and the room of escorts begins to applaud.

An escort from the back yells, "So what are you doing way down here with us? Aren't you supposed to be slaying Variables upstairs in the arena?"

Nulo realizes they don't know about his demotion and says, "Sometimes you have to give back to move forward." The escorts cheer the charitable response and Nulo takes an unmerited bow. "Thank you, guys. I had a rough morning and needed this encouragement."

"We should be thanking you," Grae says. "Every negative thing I've heard about you seems to be a lie. You are pretty cool in person."

Nulo pulls him into a playful headlock and asks, "What's your name?"

"Umm, Grae. Officer Grae."

"Well, Officer Grae, do you mind being my apprentice during this brief training?"

"Wow, really?"

Nulo wraps his arm around Grae's neck and says, "I'm getting the feeling I need somebody like you around to get me through this. So what do you say, Officer Grae?"

Grae remembers his original plan to escape and tries to back out of the deal. "I can't, I'm sorry."

"What do you mean? I'm trying to help you live out that dream. Fear and respect don't work well together."

The rest of the escorts encourage Grae by chanting, "Do it, do it, do it." Grae feels he doesn't have a choice and accepts by surrendering his hands. He walks alongside Nulo, but thinks about his backpack stashed under the desk. Grae mumbles, "I'm getting arrested for sure now."

Nulo announces to the class, "You all are in for a treat because I like you guys. I will skip over all those boring bartering tutorials and go straight to combat. This will be our little secret, so reserve your excitement while we're walking through these hallways, alright?"

They escorts nod and lightly high five one another.

CHAPTER 10

Kaphir's defiant manhunt continues on the mezzanine during his bartering shift. He angrily fires at every Variable standing in his way. He turns to one of his comrades and yells, "If you were right behind him, how did you lose him?"

He shrugs. "I'm sorry, Kay."

"And where is Josiah?"

"I don't know."

Lieutenant Opha, a few yards away, is also looking for Nulo. He swings his mace at a passing Variable and mumbles to himself, "It's not like him to skip a shift."

Suddenly, Opha is bombarded by Kaphir and his crew. "Where did your little girlfriend run off to?"

"Who?"

The crew continues to fire between questions. "Stop playing dumb. I'm talking about Nulo." Opha slides away. "Not now, Kaphir. I'm busy protecting the ship, if you don't mind."

Opha trots ahead and Kaphir follows him. "Tell me where he is and I'll leave you alone."

Nushaka overhears the discussion. "Are you looking for Nulo? I heard he got demoted and is helping out with the barter training."

Kaphir stops firing his AC and laughs. "Really?"

"Because of what happened yesterday."

"This just keeps getting better and better."

Opha watches Kaphir run off with his team and asks Nushaka, "Why would you tell him that?"

"I was just trying to help. I was going to head down there myself after our shift because he owes me something."

Opha starts to follow Kaphir, but reconsiders. "No, this is not your battle, Opha. Nulo can handle himself. Remember what happened last time."

. . . .

Lieutenant Nulo leads his escorts across a secured cylinder catwalk, points downwards and says, "Alright guys, this is the lobby level, a very dangerous level at that."

One of the escorts says, "Then they should keep you on this level, Lieutenant." Nulo chuckles. "Thanks, but it doesn't receive enough Variable traffic for me."

"How is it dangerous?"

"A lot of times, infected Leviathans slip through the shipment and ACs alone can't stop them. That's why commanders have stronger formunition."

A nasally officer looks at both side posts and asks, "The commanders work on this floor, right?"

"Yeah, that's right."

"So where are they?"

Nulo presses his face against the glass, but there is no sign of Commander Dena or Locy. "Hmm, that's weird. Maybe they are between shifts."

Grae quietly asks, "So why aren't you a maphlete, Nulo?"

"I chose not to work inside a cubical for the rest of my life."

"I totally agree and I'm kind of doing the same thing. Why upgrade to something you wouldn't like?"

"That being said, let's go do some combat."

Returning to the presidential level, Dena secretly lurks through the halls with wide eyes and soft steps. She smears her back against a wall and peeks around the lit corner. She looks for cameras and, seeing none, continues to carefully follow the GPS on her TDA. She sprints down the hallway, avoiding any maphletes who might identify her. She sighs. "First things first, I gotta find this Cove I keep hearing about."

Dena checks several windows alongside the wall and finds one loose from its casing. She wiggles it a bit, but it is locked from the inside and won't give. Dena peers inside the room, sees it's the maphlete's library. She pulls a chisel from her backpack and carves a small circle in the window. She sticks her arm through the hole and unlocks the clasp.

Dena hops from one wobbly shelf to another, trying to time her jumps and avoid triggering the floor sensors. She scans the alphabetized pillars. "Bingo."

She leaps to a drawer labeled 'Confidential' and pulls open each shelf, one by one, using the magnet bracelets for grip. She skims through the index card catalog. "I'm getting nowhere." She gives up her search, but notices a blinking cube stuck to a shelf.

She analyzes the obscure box and lightly pokes it. Dena pulls it off and smells it. "Yuck, what *is* this thing? Whatever it is, doesn't look like it's supposed to be here." She latches it to her belt and moves on. Dena somersaults onto a desk and dives in front of the exit. She feels like she is being watched and tucks herself tightly into the shadows. She raises her AC scope and switches it to thermal vision, but body heat doesn't register in the room. She twists the door handle without making a sound and swiftly moves into a hallway.

Leaving the door unlocked, she tiptoes through the hallway and hears footsteps approaching from behind. She gallops ahead and peeks around the corner. Again, she doesn't see anyone. Dena presses her ear to the ground trying to determine where the footsteps are coming from. Silence.

Dena checks her TDA and takes a chance by moving forward and hears, "Dena." She jumps, spins around, AC at the ready, saying, "Who's there?"

"Whoa, it's me, Commander," the hooded Officer Riti whispers with his hands above his head.

Dena grunts. "Riti, why would you do something like that? You almost scared the life out of me."

Riti removes his hood and laughs. "I learned yesterday that hiding from you is not the best option."

"Thank you, but … ugh." Dena smiles and tries to slow her racing heart.

Riti smirks. "What are you doing at this end of the ship?"

"I took your advice and plan on leaving the Arvelee."

Riti laughs. "Really, now? It's just not that easy, you know. You have to have a plan, like boarding and voice cards!" Riti ejects his card and holds it up to her face.

"Oh," Dena says. "And that's why I need to find the Arvelee's cove. Where is it?"

Riti gazes into Dena's eager eyes as he questions his judgment. "If you're going to do this, you need to hurry before the Tamin takes off." He flips through his TDA and shows her the coordinates. "Type this in your GPS. The Cove is inside the courtyard; adjacent to Saint Galley Axilla Bakery."

126

"Okay." Dena pauses before speaking again, "How about we leave the ship together? You know, so you can tell me everything?"

"Sure." Riti caresses Dena's cheek. "That sounds like a great idea."

Dena smiles. "Awesome."

"But first I need to say my goodbyes to an old friend. I'll meet you in the escort line down on the lobby level."

Dena agrees with a nod and continues on her journey.

. . . .

Nulo leads the escorts up a flight of stairs and finishes another heroic story.

"Are you serious?" Grae blurts. "You actually crushed a Variable's skull with your bare hands?"

"I sure did and got an extra 200 points from a few sponsors."

Nulo opens a set of doors to what he believes is the simulation room, but turns out to be the back entrance of the balcony level. From afar, Nulo sees his Iota sponsors and panics.

An escort yells, "Oooh, Nulo took us to the bistro. We get to meet some of the top elite now." The other escorts agree and cheer out loud.

"No, no, no," Nulo says. "Those are powerful phages from the Beverod who probably don't speak our language. But maybe next time I'll introduce you all with an appointment."

Grae suggests, "Can we have a tour inside the bistro at least?"

"Absolutely not. Did you guys forget that we aren't supposed to be up here? In fact, we should head back down now before someone sees us."

Unfortunately, the double doors locked behind them and they're stuck on the balcony level. Grae points past the bistro on the other side of the corridor and says, "There's a sign over there that says, 'exit'. I'm sure we can take those stairs back down."

"Alright." Nulo sighs. "But I don't want to hear a peep from any of you."

The escorts quiet themselves and prepare to walk past the Iota's bistro. Nulo slouches with the crowd of escorts and smoothly blends in. The escorts admire the Iota bystanders conversing outside the bistro's door. A few of them wave, while others secretly take pictures of the luxurious restaurant.

Grae realizes this is the perfect time to slip away and retrieve his backpack. He improvises and bends down to tie his shoe in front of the bistro. The crowd of escorts walks around Grae and continues to follow Nulo. Grae stands and spots his old friend, Obatrius, inside the bistro. He whispers, "What is he doing up here?"

Nulo reiterates, "Right this way." He holds the door open and high-fives each passing escort. Finally, Nulo notices Grae entering the bistro doors. "No!" Nulo shouts. He turns to the rest of the escorts and says with urgency, "Stay right here, guys, I think we just lost Officer Grae." Knowing he cannot afford another demerit, Nulo runs after him.

.   .   .   .

Crawling through an airshaft, Commander Dena opens a vent and lowers herself into a room. She whispers, "Where am I?" She looks around and sees many labelled boxes stacked in the storage room. She reads a label above a bar code, St. Galley Axilla Bakery. "Okay. I'm sort of in the right place."

Cautiously opening the storage door, she smoothly blends in with the bakery customers. She exits the store and enters the busy courtyard of pedestrians and hears her GPS chime. "You have arrived at your destination." Dena looks around, but only sees the storefronts of Sharlo's Diner and St. Galley Axilla Bakery as options. "I hope he gave me the correct coordinates."

Dena notices the caution tape and broken glass on the ground from Sharlo's door and says, "This definitely looks like it could be the place."

She steps through the open door frame and scans the vacant diner. Sharlo yells from the back, "I'm sorry, but we're closed today." Unaware of yesterday's events, Dena continues into the diner and approaches Sharlo as she is sweeping debris into a dustpan.

"What happened in here?"

"You know, the usual. Men being men. How can I help you?"

"I'm sort of new to this. I'm looking for the Cove?"

Shocked by Dena's complete naiveté or bold defiance, Sharlo continues cleaning up. "I'm sorry, but I don't know what that is or what you are talking about."

Dena, ignorant of the Cove's secrecy, pleads with Sharlo. "I heard it's a place where we can buy items on the black market."

Sharlo quickly pushes Dena towards the exit. "Nope, never heard of it."

"Well, I was told that there was a--"

Sharlo cuts Dena off. "You must have your coordinates confused. This is just a diner and I'm the owner."

"Are you sure? A friend of mine gave me these. "

"Well, you need to go back to your friend and tell them they need to give you all the facts first."

Dena walks into the center of the courtyard and spins in a complete circle searching for any place that could be the Cove. Suddenly, Dena is nudged from behind. "Miss me?"

Dena jumps and whips around frantic. She rolls her eyes unimpressed once she sees its Locy. "Oh, hey."

"*Oh, hey*?" Locy repeats. "I thought you'd be a little more excited to see me. What, you don't want me to come with you anymore?"

Dena twists her lips. "Are you *really* coming with me?"

"I guess I have to now, since we both walked away from our jobs to find this Aberash."

"Thank you." Dena emotionally pulls Locy in for a hug. "How did you even find me?"

"I ran into your *friend* Riti and he told me everything."

Dena chuckles. "Yes he's *just* a friend. Stop giving me that look like you know something."

"I know the two of you were planning on leaving the Arvelee. Hmm, sounds like I've already been replaced."

Dena smiles. "No one could ever replace your crazy self."

Locy jokes. "And you're still calling me crazy. Thank you."

"You know what I mean, shut up. Hey do you know anything about a black market around here? I asked the lady in Sharlo's and she had no idea what I was talking about."

Locy whispers, "It's called the black market for a reason, Dena. Follow me and keep your mouth shut."

. . . .

Nulo hides his face and mingles with a loud crew of Iota members outside the balcony area. He slides away unseen and slips past the chatting maître de at the front podium. He quickly grabs a hanging hat to cover his face and enters the bistro to find Grae.

The room is full of rowdy business owners, clingy paramours and cigar smoke. Nulo carefully searches the room full of high-class social gamblers. He weaves through laughing, drunk phages and hears his name being brutally tossed around.

"He sucks."

"I have 100,000 points on Nulo."

"I'll raise you 200,000 he doesn't hit half that."

"Nulo's not even down there."

"I heard he's sick and took the day off."

"Sick? I heard he got demoted."

"I give Nulo two more years until he's washed up."

"And I'll say 50,000 points in one year."

Nulo frantically covers his face and bumps into a crossing waitress. "I'm sorry."

The waitress recognizes him and he lightly places a finger over her lips. "Shh, please." She nods and Nulo takes one of her menus to shield his face.

Grae spots Obatrius grabbing drinks at the bar and walks over to him. Obatrius spins around with his platter and almost runs into him. "Grae?" Obatrius fearfully asks, "What are you doing up here in the bistro?"

Grae retorts, "What are you doing here? Everyone's been talking about you. You okay?"

"No." Obatrius pulls Grae to the side. "You shouldn't have come here. Get as far away as you can before they see us talking."

"What are you talking about?"

Paranoid, Obatrius asks, "Are you still selling those cards?"

Grae answers, "Yeah, but I'm planning on jumping ships and starting over. You should come with me."

"It's over. The Iotas are not who they once were anymore. Save your cards for the upcoming war."

"War? Wait, slow down. What do you mean?"

"Hey!" Nulo shoves Grae from behind. "We have to get out of here right now."

"Get off me," Grae demands. "I'm not going anywhere until I'm done talking to my friend."

"Who?"

Grae turns around and Obatrius has disappeared. Grae rushes back to the floor and looks through the crossing Iota members. "He was just right here, the waiter."

Nulo knows at any moment somebody will recognize him. He desperately grabs Grae. "Come on!"

Grae yanks his arm back. "Will you stop touching me?"

Nulo is stunned by Grae's sudden boldness. "Who do you think you are talking to, youngster?"

"I'm talking to you, Nulo! I'm taking your advice and getting my respect today. So back off before you make things worse."

Nulo roughs up Grae's collar. "Who are you? Are you one of those spies or something?"

"Oooh and the *plot* thickens!" A familiar voice interrupts their conversation.

Nulo turns and sees Kaphir approaching while his goons cover the exits of the bistro.

"Cretchit." Nulo pleads, "Please Kaphir, not up here."

"This isn't your choice, super soldier." Kaphir gives his followers a hand signal. "Let's get this started, fellas."

They secretly pull the Nicil alarm and Kaphir yells through a bullhorn, "Please exit the balcony in an orderly fashion. There is a tiny hole in the glass and as a precaution we need you all out of this area before the next Nicil hits." The elite inside the balcony's bistro begin to pack up their belongings and evacuate.

Nulo quickly catches on to Kaphir's plan and tries to blend in with the rest. "Hey!" Kaphir hugs Nulo. "Not so fast, super soldier. I want you to stick around for the best part."

As the elite begin to thin out, Nulo leans over to Grae. "If you're not with these hoodlums, I suggest you leave like the rest."

Confused, Grae asks, "What's going on?"

"Just get out of here and catch up with the rest of the escorts."

Kaphir playfully responds, "Aww, come on. Don't be so hard on the boy. All he wants is to see a good fight."

Nulo pleads, "Kaphir, please, I don't want him a part of this. Just let him out. Our differences have nothing to do with him."

Kaphir contemplates, and signals his men to unlock the door. Grae is shoved towards the exit and sees the fear in Nulo's eyes. Grae is pushed all the way out and hears hearty laughter behind the closed door.

133

"That was dumb," Kaphir says. "Not only did you insist that he leave, but you failed to take his working arm cannon."

Nulo cracks his neck and says, "I'd rather fight fair."

Kaphir counts his henchmen. "Fair? It looks you're down four to one."

"Wasn't there five of you earlier? Oops."

Kaphir pieces together what happened to Josiah and applauds. "Wow, impressive, and for someone who's hilariously helpless, you still have a confident mouth."

"I'm just being honest. None of you can beat me in a fair fight. Especially you, Kaphir. That's why you brought these idiots with you."

Kaphir inserts customized ammunition one by one into his AC and turns it up to its maximum power. He laughs. "Naw, they're just my audience."

"You had an audience. Your crew ran them out, remember?"

"Naw those were witnesses, if you get what I'm saying."

Sarcastically, Nulo says, "So shooting a helpless phage is worth bragging to your friends about? Hmm, that sounds really macho. Okay so if this your thing, go right ahead and do what you gotta do." Nulo locks his fingers behind his head and adds, "Just make sure you shoot me right in the back like a real soldier."

Members of Kaphir's crew look at one another as their consciences begin to speak.

"He's right, Kaphir, let's just go. We scared him enough."

Kaphir continues to hold up his cannon during the period of silence. Rebellious, Kaphir opens fire into Nulo's spine. Nulo is propelled into the wall, causing the steel roof to collapse on top of him.

Kaphir taunts, "You thought that little speech was going to work on me? You thought all of a sudden I had respect for you? Ha. *Just make sure you shoot me in the back like a real soldier*. It just dawned on me how pathetic you are. You're weak and I'm tired of this ship praising you." Kaphir spikes a boulder from the wall on Nulo's knee and steps on it to add more pressure. As Nulo reaches for the rock, Kaphir kicks him in the ribs.

"Stay down! You said you wanted a one-on-one fight right? Well come on super soldier, let's see what you got." Kaphir pulls Nulo from the wreckage and body slams him against the ballistic glass.

"Argh!" Nulo yells.

The glass vibrates loud enough for Opha to hear from his arena vantage point. He looks up and sees Kaphir's silhouette striking another person. Opha assumes the worst for his friend.

As Nulo attempts to crawl away, Kaphir uses a chair to uppercut him in the chin.

"Stop!" A crony speaks up, "I think he's had enough Kaphir."

Kaphir whips around and yells, "It's enough when I say it is." He stomps Nulo repeatedly in the stomach and kicks him in the throat.

"Kaphir, relax, he's still a lieutenant. Do you want to get purged for killing him?"

Kaphir steps away from Nulo, breathing heavily and signals to his goons. "Now get him up on his knees."

As Nulo is lifted out of his pool of blood, Kaphir rips off his TDA glove. He holds the glove with two hands and bats it against Nulo's face. Nulo howls from the abuse and curls into a ball.

Kaphir activates the camera on his TDA and scans an image of Nulo's disfigured face. "I'm gonna make sure everybody sees their beloved soldier at his best."

Unremorseful, Kaphir begins trashing Nulo's TDA. "Let's see how fast you heal when you don't have one of these." Kaphir finishes the glove by breaking it over his knee and shattering it into pieces. From afar, Kaphir sees the class of escorts watching the fight inside the bistro. Kaphir takes Nulo's bloody jaw and points it towards the frightened escorts. "Hey look, Lieutenant, your students salute your hard work on the Arvelee. Take a bow for them, super soldier." Kaphir then whispers in Nulo's ear, "*Now I accept your apology.*" He signals for his shaken crew to follow him through the exit.

The escorts wait until Kaphir's entourage are gone and run to Nulo's hemorrhaging body.

"Are you okay? Lieutenant?"

Nulo says, barely above a whisper, "Thought I told ya'll to stay put." He gags on his blood before passing out.

"No!" An escort rolls Nulo onto his side to prevent him from choking. Nulo falls into a seizure state. His eyes roll up into his head and his muscles lock all over.

A few escorts desperately try to restrain him. They start gathering their resuscitation cards, not knowing his TDA has been destroyed.

"Where's his glove?"

"Doesn't matter, I'm giving him mine." One escort pulls his off and attempts to slide it on Nulo's left forearm. He tugs, but Nulo's stiff fingers snag on the glove due to his seizing. Others join in. They yank the TDA harder and a concerned officer yells, "Stop. You're going to break his fingers."

"Does anybody have muscle relaxers?"

"Where's Grae?"

"Everybody move." A chubby escort climbs over and pours a handful of pills into Nulo's mouth.

A female officer asks, "Are those muscle relaxers?"

"No, they're X5 capsules."

"Energy pills?"

"Yes. Do we have any other options? Let's just hope the adrenaline helps with the pain."

Lieutenant Opha exits the balcony's elevator, hoping he's in the right area. He follows the posted signs for Balcony's Bistro and sprints down a narrow hallway. He runs into a dead end. "Where is it?"

"Help!"

Opha turns toward the far end of the hallway and finds a few wandering escorts scattered around. "What's happening up here?"

"Follow us, Lieutenant. Nulo needs your help."

Opha follows the escorts down another hallway and finally finds the bistro. Opha bursts through the entrance and sees a small cluster of escorts weeping at the far end. "Oh, no. No, no," Opha says. "Let me through. I'm here to help." The escorts spread apart and Opha sees a lifeless Nulo with no sign of recovery.

"You're too late," an officer says. "Nulo is dead."

Opha pulls out his jar of resuscitation cream and rubs a thick layer all over Nulo's cuts and bruises. He massages it deep into his purple skin. "Come on, buddy, get up." The cream seeps deep inside his pores causing Nulo's birthmark to glow and heal from the inside out.

"Give him some room, stand back."

Nulo moans and blinks his eyes. The female officer shouts, "He's alive!" Nulo grunts and coughs uncontrollably. He tries to focus and squints at the sight of Opha. The escorts stand clear and continue to cheer Nulo's resurrection.

Opha helps Nulo to a seated position and asks, "You okay, buddy?"

Nulo doesn't waste any time placing blame. "Buddy? All of this happened because of you." Opha holds up his resuscitation cream confused. "I just saved your life."

"You wouldn't have had to if you didn't stop me in the stairwell earlier. That's how they found me."

"No. The girl you were with told them where to find you."

"Why didn't you try to stop them or warn me they were coming?"

"You kept me in the dark. How was I supposed to know this would happen?"

Nulo speaks angrily. "You knew. All this is your way of paying me back from yesterday."

"You think I set this up? How dare you try to pin this on me? Even when I help you, I still get punished. I can't win with you Nulo."

"You're right. You'll never win because you're a registered loser." Nulo, unable to stand up, hunches over. "From this point on, we are no longer friends. I don't need yours or anybody else's help. You all are dead weight to me."

"What?"

"Move." Nulo limps through the idle escorts and exits the balcony's bistro.

. . . .

"Are you sure this is the place?" Dena asks Locy, while standing in front of the Cove's entrance.

"Yes." She continues to try another combination of numbers on the keypad to unlock the door.

Dena asks, "How long does this take?"

"Stop talking and let me think." Locy stares at the ten digits and whispers out other options.

The antsy Dena continues, "Are we even allowed in here?"

"No, so shut up. Hold on, I think I remember it now." Locy slowly types in a four digit code and they both hear the door unlock.

Locy winks. "I told you." She struts in while Dena cautiously peeks through the doorway. Unimpressed by the slums, Dena says, "This place doesn't look anything like I imagined."

"What were you expecting? Gold countertops and glass display cases?"

"Uh, yeah."

Locy laughs and rings the bell on to the counter. "Hello?"

"Who runs this filthy place?" Dena whispers.

"I don't remember his name, but the last time I was here it was an old skinny man with a full beard."

Dena wipes dust with her finger. "Well, if he's planning on keeping customers, he should hire some sort of help to clean up the place."

Suddenly, a sweaty Nulo bursts inside the Cove. "Doc! Doc, where are you?"

Dr. Ribonu finally comes out from the storage area with tinted goggles over his eyes. "I'm here, what is it?" Ribonu sees Nulo's dreadful appearance and pouts. "Oh, not again. What happened this time?"

"That's not important," Nulo answers. "But I desperately need to buy some gloves."

"What for?"

Nulo snaps at Ribonu, "I thought you said you don't ask questions? Just give me what I asked for."

Locy stands in between the two and says, "Uh, excuse me? But we were here first."

Ribonu turns to Locy. "I'm sorry, ladies, I didn't know you were ready to order."

"We are, and we're in kind of a hurry."

Nulo retorts, "Well can it wait? Because I'm a regular here."

Locy yells, "I don't care if you're Captain Lyme with a broken wrist, we were here first and he's gonna help us first."

Nulo leans his disfigured face towards Locy. "Look at me. Who do you think should be helped *first*?"

Locy points her AC at Nulo's neck and says, "We should, unless you want me to finish off your face. Now back off and wait your turn."

Nulo slaps her arm away. "Do you know who I am?"

Ribonu steps in. "That's enough, you two."

"Yeah, calm down, Locy." Dena adds. "He's not worth it." Dena quickly hands Ribonu their list of expected items. "We need everything on there."

Ribonu looks over the list. "Okay, let me gather it up for you." Ribonu notices Locy and Nulo are having an undaunted stare off. Ribonu repeats, "I said that's enough."

Nulo storms down an aisle grumbling and kicks a stack of boxes.

Locy asks Ribonu, "Are you gonna let that idiot tear your place apart like that?"

Laughing, Dena whispers, "I'm sure he doesn't mind."

Nulo looks down in the mess and notices one of the boxes has custom gloves buried in Styrofoam.

Dr. Ribonu answers, "He'll be fine." He pulls out cards and says, "Here's your boarding and resus and I just need to grab your image card from the back."

Nulo watches Ribonu returns to the back room and quietly rummages through the boxes he kicked over. He finds an arm cannon buried in the Styrofoam and attempts to steal it.

Locy watches his every move and purposely shouts, "Hey are you buying that?"

Busted, Nulo says, "Yes, Commander Nosey, Commander Stuck-Up. Ribonu's a friend of mine."

"So why did you wait until your *friend* went in the back?"

"So I can be ready when – you know what? I don't have to answer to you."

Before Locy can respond the Cove's lights flicker, then completely cut off.

Dena yells out, "What's happening? Locy are you doing this?"

"No not this time," Locy fearfully answers.

The entire ship quakes as they hear shelves fall to the ground. The three struggle to keep their balance as the lights gradually returns.

Locy says, "That felt like a Nicil. What are the lieutenants doing up there?"

"Another bomb?" Dena asks frazzled on the ground. "That would be two in two days."

Nulo grabs a portable tablet from a random box and walks to the rear of the room. He turns it on and plugs it into a socket. "Exactly what I thought it was" Nulo proclaims. "These idiots just released an EMP because I'm not in the arena."

Locy asks, "And what's that?"

"It's an electromagnetic pulse bomb, Commander Nosey."

"This is why I'm leaving, because of men like you."

143

Covering with an awkward laugh, Dena rephrases her statement, "What she meant to say is, 'this is why I left a man like you'. We're not going anywhere."

Dr. Ribonu finally returns, apologizing. "Sorry for the delay. The blackout kind of ruined my organization back there." He hands Dena the image cards and says, "Everything will be 21,500 q-points."

Without hesitation, Dena whips her TDA beneath the barter scanner and pays for it.

Spitefully, Locy leans towards Dr. Ribonu. "While you were in the back your *friend* was about to steal an AC until I stopped him."

"Liar!" Nulo charges Locy with a closed fist.

"Don't you dare, Nulo!" Ribonu says. "Leave her alone."

Dena pulls Locy towards the exit and pushes her completely out of the door. Dena says, "I'm so sorry. We're gone and you'll never hear from us again."

As the door closes, Nulo mumbles, "And I hope to never see the two of you, either." He explains to Ribonu, "You see the type of respect I got on this ship? None. This is why I need this TDA and AC activated now."

"Slow down. I can't send you on a killing spree just yet."

Nulo sighs. "Doc I don't have time for another one of your lectures. I just need these two gloves activated so I can be on my way."

"What's gotten into you? Where is all this bitterness coming from?"

"It's always been there, but only my *friends* would've seen it."

Shocked, Ribonu shrugs. "So I'm not your friend because I'm not giving you what you want? If you knew what I knew, I am the last person who you want to cut ties with."

Nulo understands his disadvantage and softly murmurs, "Sorry." He pulls the gloves onto his forearm and finishes assembling them.

Ribonu pleads, "Look, I don't know what happened or what you have planned, but it's time for you to be the bigger person. Just walk away."

Nulo ignores him. "Just activate my gloves."

Disgusted, Ribonu shakes his head at Nulo's stubbornness. Ribonu pulls out a tool and begrudgingly begins to program the gloves. He inserts two tiny generators inside both gloves and says, "If this is where we stand, so be it. I see that right now that you are too far gone for my help anyway." The gloves turn on and Nulo says, "That is the first thing you and I can both agree on." Nulo inserts three resus cards into his TDA and grabs a handful of formunition cartridges. He notices Ribonu has activated his arm cannon with an exclusive motherboard.

"You're giving me a mark 5 arm cannon?" Nulo blurts. "The whole ship is still operating on the 4th generation. Is this some sort of a joke?"

"Not at all," Ribonu says. "I'm giving you what you want. Today marks the day that Nulo gets to chase his selfish behavior without repercussion. But I'm telling you from experience, this won't end well."

"You can't talk me out of this one, Doc. I am in too deep. I can't let these fools run around the ship thinking I'm an easy win. I'm the best on board and I have to make sure everybody knows."

"So this is what it's all about? Your pride?"

"Yup and I guess I'm a sucker to see how it all ends." Nulo tightens the straps on both gloves and preps to leave.

Ribonu sheds a tear and quietly suggests, "Please, Nulo, listen for the voices. They will guide you back to the Aberash."

Nulo sucks his teeth and stubbornly ignores the advice. Ribonu watches Nulo walk out of the Cove without ever looking back.

CHAPTER 11

Gasping for air, Grae returns to the classroom. He flips over the desk where he hid his backpack and yanks the chair away. To his surprise, it is gone. "Cretchit. I knew I shouldn't have left it here."

Grae punches the chalkboard and hears a female voice call out, "Looking for this, Mr. Card Dealer?"

He looks up and sees Fotaria dangling his backpack by the doorway. "Fotaria? What are you doing here? I thought you'd be gone already."

Fotaria sighs. "You still owe me that free bartering card, remember?"

Grae laughs. "You were supposed to show up at my place for that deal."

"I did, but by the time I got there your place was ransacked."

Grae mumbles, "Yeah, some Iota spy tried to set me up, but I got out of there just in time."

"Looks like you need this vacation more than I do. Can I still get that free card if I tag along with you?"

"You sure can." Grae hugs her tightly and exhales. "And thank you for not being so quick to judge me."

"No, thank you. Thank you for giving me a second chance to start over." Fotaria kisses Grae on the cheek and leads him out of the classroom.

While approaching the elevator, Grae explains, "In order to ensure our safety, we have to be off the Arvelee with the Tamin barter."

"Okay, when does it start?"

"It just did. And from experience, it'll be safer to exit through the lobby and blend in as an escort."

"Are you kidding me?" Fotaria asks. "At this hour, the lobby will be swarmed with Iota commanders. If we want to get across smoothly, the

147

mezzanine is the way to go. Trust me, I've been working this system for years and know all the loopholes."

Grae smiles. "Well then, lead the way." He hands her the bartering card and steps onto the elevator. Once it reaches the mezzanine level, Fotaria presses the button. "The door isn't opening."

Grae walks over to inspect. He laughs. "Well, there's our problem, you were pressing the close button."

Embarrassed, Fotaria sighs. "I'm so stupid. I think my nerves are starting to kick in."

Grae lifts her chin. "There's no need to be nervous. Remember what I told you in the promenade. I'll protect you." The elevator doors shoot open and they immediately run into a cluster of foot traffic. Grae takes Fotaria by the hand and pulls her through the crowd. "We have to get past this rush and into the escorting line as soon as possible."

Grae steps into the mob, zigzags and shoves his way through. Fotaria releases Grae's hand, but continues to follow his path. She loses sight of Grae when a towering soldier dashes in between them. "Just keep going. I'm right behind you." As she shuffles through, a flood of cheering soldiers carries her petite body further away from Grae.

Through her hidden earpiece, Fotaria hears, "You're losing him. Find him before it is too late."

She responds, "I'm trying the best I can."

"Well, it's not good enough."

Fotaria pushes her way back, but struggles through more crossing pedestrians.

Grae checks the time on his TDA and shuffles between more soldiers. So focused on getting across, Grae fails to check on Fotaria. Assuming she's still behind him, he yells over his shoulder, "We're almost there."

Fotaria is thrown to the ground by the influx. She squirms on her back to avoid the stampede and yells, "I'm down, and I lost him." Two trailing maphletes arrive to help Fotaria back to her feet.

Suddenly Sultri arrives furious. "You disgrace me."

"I'm sorry," she pleads. "I really tried to catch him this time."

Sultri grips the back of Fotaria's neck. "You didn't! You had one job and both times you let him go. Don't you understand that my life is on the line?"

"How was I supposed to know he was going to jump out of the window? I told you exactly where we would be and you all blew it."

"No, the plan was to keep him on the elevator until I got there. What happened?"

"I didn't want to look suspicious. Look, we know he's heading to the escorting line so we'll just catch him there." Sultri agrees by rolling his eyes.

Grae eventually reaches the other side and doesn't see Fotaria behind him. "You gotta be kidding me." He scans the passing heads and frantically searches for her. He sees a glimpse of a maphlete escorting Fotaria back into the elevator. He grunts. "Cretchit." He contemplates on saving her, but checks the bartering time. "So much for my protecting her." He shakes off his sadness and moves inside the line.

. . . .

149

Lieutenant Opha exits the mezzanine elevator and jogs back to the arena to complete his shift. Esko is waiting near the entrance and says, "I'm glad to see you decided to come back."

"Wait, I can explain."

Esko folds his arms and says, "Yeah, explain to me why you left your shift before it was over."

"I had to rush up to the balcony because I saw Nulo getting attacked."

"Enough," Esko yells. "Stop lying to me. Nulo got demoted yesterday and there is no way he could've been in the balcony."

"Go see for yourself. And ask those frightened escorts who are still in there."

"No need because Kaphir told me the truth."

"The truth?"

Lieutenant Kaphir limps into sight, exaggerating an injury. Kaphir explains to Esko, "I'm sorry. I tried to stop Opha from leaving, but he struck me unconscious."

Opha chuckles and turns to Esko and says, "You can't honestly believe this guy. I followed him because he was looking for Nulo. He's the reason I left."

Esko says, "Your stories aren't adding up."

Opha points to a nearby camera and yells, "Check the surveillance and you'll get the real story there."

"We can't," Esko says. "All the cameras went down recently. Someone triggered an EMP and scrambled the hard drives."

Opha looks over at Kaphir, who winks at him. Opha lunges forward and chokes Kaphir against the wall, "You're setting me up!"

Esko pulls Opha off and yells, "Back off!"

Opha pleads, "I wouldn't do anything to hurt the Arvelee and you know that."

"You're right, but somebody has to take the blame and all evidence points to you. I'm sorry, Opha, but you need to turn yourself in for investigation."

"Investigation? Are you kidding?"

"Not at all, Lieutenant!"

Esko deactivates Opha's AC and attaches magnetic rings around both of his gloves. Two other maphletes arrive and escorts Opha to an interrogation room on the presidential level. Kaphir stays behind, making taunting faces and blowing a kiss to Opha.

. . . .

Grae causally blends into the escorting line with his head tucked low. While he estimates the length of the line, a crossing escort tackles him. Grae's book bag falls off his shoulder and slides to the feet of a menacing maphlete. The maphlete asks, "Is there a reason why you're taking personal items during this bartering exchange?"

Grae improvises. "I was running late to my shift and didn't have time to leave it in the locker room."

The maphlete stares into Grae's watery eyes and says, "I'll let you slide, but I'm taking your bag. Come get it when your shift ends." Grae panics, but graciously nods his head. Without checking what's inside, the maphlete takes off with his heel rockets in the opposite direction.

Grae exhales. Hopefully he'd be long gone before they figured out what was in that bag.

Grae grabs his MEG case with the rest of the escorts and slowly proceeds forward.

"Hey, Grae? Psst!" He finally hears his name being whispered and checks behind him. Grae sees Sultri in a disguise a few escorts back.

Confused, but filled with joy, Grae meets him. "Sultri, I heard you were dead. You really had me worried last time we talked."

Sultri laughs. "I'm good now, but I gotta get off this ship. Hey listen, do you have an extra boarding card I can use until we get across? I promise to pay you back in time."

"Keep your voice down," Grae whispers. "And the answer is no. My bag was taken by a maphlete not too long ago."

Sultri gets closer. "Do you have any other cards on you that I can buy?"

Insulted, Grae pushes Sultri away. "I just told you what happened. Why are you acting so weird right now?"

Sultri presses his earpiece and reports, "You said that was good enough? Copy."

Suddenly, the earlier maphlete returns with Grae's bag.

Now putting everything together, Grae aggressively mugs Sultri in the face. "You set me up?"

"I sure did and every bit of it was worth it."

The maphlete strikes Grae with a baton and restrains him to the ground. Still devastated, Grae cries out, "Why Sultri, why? After all the favors I did for you. I thought we were friends."

"Friends wouldn't try to start a new life with my girlfriend just because you thought I was dead." Sultri calls Fotaria out from hiding. "Take a bow baby. You have just apprehended one of the Arvelee's most wanted."

Forced to smile, Fotaria watches the sour-looking Grae being escorted out of the line and onto his interrogation.

Disgusted, Grae shakes his head. "Ha, I knew my luck was too good to be true."

. . . .

Ironically, Dena and Locy are in the same line a few escorts ahead of Grae. They overhear the charges and panic. Dena hides her bag under her shirt and says, "We gotta find another way across."

Locy agrees and says, "Follow me." She pulls Dena out of the line and cuts through an idle crowd of escorts. Locy avoids bumping into crossing pedestrians and maneuvers the crowd with precision.

Dena second-guesses their decision and asks, "Are you certain we're going to make it?"

"No," Locy says. "But we can't afford to take any chances in that line with our bag of illegal cards."

. . . .

The elevator door opens and a frustrated Maphlete Ghii enters the presidential level. He marches down the brightly lit hallways, passing several interrogation rooms filled with accused phages. Ghii enters the last suite and finds Director Arooni resting in the lounge. Maphlete Ghii pauses. "Director, I just got word we have Lieutenant Opha coming up for questioning."

Arooni rubs her temple. "Opha? I'm sorry, Ghii, but you're going to have to refresh my memory."

"Opha was Nulo's accomplice in the Nicil bomb incident yesterday."

Arooni nods. "Aye, Opha. Right, right. Now that he's coming, I need you to release Nulo from suspension and have them both report to inquiry suite 2A."

Ghii hesitates. "Umm."

Arooni frowns. "Is there a problem?"

"Yeah, kind of, ma'am. We never suspended Nulo and now he's um… missing."

Arooni jumps up. "He's what?"

"Esko and I made the executive decision to demote him to a temporary position as a punishment and…"

"Demoted him?" Arooni yells. "I specifically said to hold him in suspension until I figured out what to do with him. Nothing more."

"We voted and thought it would be best suited that Nulo learned his lesson by removing his arm cannon."

Arooni sarcastically states, "Oh, so you're *Captain* Ghii now?"

"Not at all," Ghii answers with a tight lip.

"Maybe it's Director Ghii?"

Ghii sighs. "No, it's just Maphlete Ghii."

"That's right," Arooni yells. "Your job is to take orders from the Director. Me. I am the superior maphlete of this ship and you deliberately disobeyed my orders."

Paxo runs inside the suite. "Arooni."

"What?" Arooni yells.

Paxo lowers his voice and cautiously says, "Sorry, but I think the Arvelee is under attack by something."

Arooni answers without making eye contact. "I've already been notified. I have maphletes all over it."

154

Paxo interjects, "It's something else, something from the inside. The engine's temperature has peaked, is unstable and beyond system resets."

Arooni folds her arms. "Have you checked with the boiler room supervisor?"

"Yes and there wasn't anything out of the ordinary."

Maphlete Ghii steps in to explain. "It's because of the EMP. Our defense sensors were too low to recover."

Director Arooni gives Ghii a long shocked stare and asks, "A second bomb was dropped?"

"Yes," Ghii says. "But that had nothing to do with us. Someone must've hotwired it. Luckily it was just an EMP and it only knocked out the hard drives."

"Luckily?" Arooni looks at the monitors. "Our ship runs on seventy-five percent electricity, which is still filtering out the Nicil mist we released yesterday. We still have soldiers in the arena and those vents could release at any time."

"I'm sorry. We thought it would be…"

"Not your problem, Ghii. You need to leave the thinking to me." Arooni pulls Ghii down by his collar and asks, "You think you can do what I do? You think you can do my job better?"

Ghii doesn't answer with words, but answers in the form of a confident expression.

Arooni grins and calmly makes a request over her TDA. "Attention, all personnel. I need Ghii, Esko and Opha all to report to inquiry suite 2A immediately."

Ghii yells in Arooni's face, "What did I do?"

155

Arooni pokes Ghii in the chest and says, "Do what I said or find yourself scrubbing floors in every bathroom this ship offers. And find me Nulo while you're at."

Paxo leads Arooni out of the suite and back down the hallway. As soon as they're out of sight, Ghii punches a deep dent into a metal locker. "I hate her," he blurts. "If she only knew."

"Hate is a strong word, my dear maphlete."

Ghii looks to see Captain Lyme grinning beside him.

Startled by her sudden appearance, Ghii respectfully bows. "I'm sorry, Captain. I didn't know anyone else was in here. Please forgive me."

"No need to apologize for your honesty. You did what you thought was right. If you could, would you go back and change anything?"

Ghii lifts his bowed head. "No, I wouldn't. I think what we did was the best way to handle Nulo."

Captain Lyme walks over and pats him on the shoulder. "Never give up with what you believe in. Always do what's right because your judgments will soon be tested. I believe in you." Lyme walks out of the lounge and leaves Ghii frozen by her prophetic wisdom.

. . . .

Lieutenant Kaphir continues to display an exaggerated limp to the passing civilians in the hallway for sympathy. Lieutenant Nushaka stops Kaphir as he passes.

"What happened to you?"

Kaphir holds his rib cage and grunts. "Ah, I found Nulo and kind of got into a little something with him and Opha, but I'll live."

"Did they jump you?"

156

Kaphir acts frightened and whispers, "You know what? I think I've said too much. Just forget I said anything to you." Kaphir limps away from the concerned Nushaka, leaving her with fuel to spread the rumor. She does not waste any time and mass messages what she has witnessed.

Kaphir lifts his TDA. "Everything is going as planned. I'll see you soon." He chuckles and hangs up. Kaphir makes it to a secure area of the ship, free from any witnesses and stops limping. He continues to walk with a confident gait and pages his crew. "Meet me at the suite in ten minutes, copy?"

A piercing sound of static blasts into Kaphir's ear and forces him to snatch the earpiece away. "What was that?" Kaphir remains calm and heads to his secured destination as planned.

Kaphir arrives and slows down when he sees his entire crew tied up and unconscious. Circumspectly, Kaphir runs to his beaten friends waiting at the doorstep of their hideout. "No, no, no." Kaphir says. He gingerly unties his tightly bound crew and whispers, "Cretchit, who did this to you?" Kaphir looks around for any helpful clues.

He hears a faint moan from one and rips the gag from his mouth. "What happened to you?" Kaphir slaps his drowsy jaw and hears a choking whisper he can't make out. "What? Who?" His moaning crewmember passes out in his arms before answering his questions. "Cretchit!" Kaphir panics and punches the wall out of rage. He stands up and looks down both ends of the hallway, but doesn't see anything suspicious.

Kaphir looks back down and does a double take. Under the arm of one of his guys, he sees an envelope with his name on it. He bends down to grab it and quickly rips it open.

Dear Lieutenant Eye Patch,

I accidentally made a mess down here in your secret hideout. So I did us both a favor and took out the trash. Sincerely, Super Soldier ☺

Kaphir balls up the note. "Nulo."

CHAPTER 12

Sharlo knocks on the entrance of the Cove. "Hey Doc, did you get my message?" She doesn't hear a response and types in the passcode to enter. Sharlo walks into a pitch-black room and yells, "Hey Doc, you okay?"

Ribonu clears his throat and whispers, "I'm over here."

Sharlo carefully steps through the dark in the direction of Ribonu's voice. Ribonu sparks a palm of fire to illuminate the room. "Sharlo, this was not the plan."

She sighs. "I know, but what did you expect so soon?"

"For the Aberash to take control of his heart and lead us back to power."

With bold discretion, Sharlo reveals, "Does he know we're Iota?"

"No. I couldn't tell him."

"Forgive me for saying this, Doc, but I don't think Nulo is the one we're looking for."

"Sharlo, you don't understand. If you look beyond his tough visage, you can see greatness and leadership. This man is so close to the Aberash, it scares me. These past couple days just confirmed the prophecy. These are the last days, and now it's time to rebuild our team."

"How are we supposed to start a team when no one has any interest of the Aberash or what we are about to face?"

"We don't have a choice. The chain of events is moving quickly and we have to act now. Contact Lieutenant Opha and bring him back to the Cove."

. . . .

159

Commander Dena arrives in the concourse of the mezzanine and navigates through the hallway. Shortly after, Locy enters gasping for breath and struggling to keep up. "Stop," Locy yells to Dena as she approaches the entrance.

Dena jerks her glove away from the scanner. "Why?"

"We're AWOL from our post remember? As soon as we scan our TDA, the maphletes will know where we are. We've got to find safer way to the barter docks."

"You're right. So what are we gonna do?"

Locy pulls out the Arvelee's blueprint and runs her finger over a few options. "The safest way is the also the longest way. And the quickest way, unfortunately, is through this arena."

"Can't we just travel through the exterior chutes?"

Locy reviews the option. "That's too risky. That's the same chute they fire off the Nicil bombs."

"I got it!" Dena's eyes widen. "Let's *still* enter here and use the lieutenants as a distraction. While we're inside, we can pick up a few q-points from Variables kills because I'm sure we're going to need them. By the time our kills are calculated with the ship, we'll be long gone on the Tamin."

Locy shrugs. "Good plan, but we still need to get inside without alerting a maphlete."

"Just wait." Dena laughs. "There is always a late lieutenant on this ship."

Before she can finish her sentence, a drowsy soldier appears behind Locy. "Look, I told you."

Locy smirks. "Here we go. It'll just be like old times when we were young, sharp-shooting lieutenants."

The lethargic lieutenant pardons himself and scans his TDA at the arena entrance. The soldier rushes in and Locy holds the door open for Dena and says, "After you."

Dena laughs and opens fire at an approaching Variable. She charges in, rolls over the back of a falling lieutenant and fires again from a kneeling position.

Locy takes out Variable scratching near the ceiling and yells, "I forgot how fun this used to be."

"I was just thinking the same thing."

"Let's raise the stakes. Whoever has less Variable kills has to pay for all of our meals until we get to the Beverod. Are you down?"

"Yeah, but that's a random prize."

"Are you as hungry as I am?"

"No, I ate before I left my room."

"Well, I'm starving and I desperately need for you to spot me a few hundred points."

"Sure, right after you win." Dena cuts off Locy's arm cannon and takes off running.

"Cheater!"

. . . .

Lieutenant Nulo escapes Kaphir by sneaking inside a door that reads *Personnel Only*. The room is smoky with low lights and surrounded by two-story engines. The wave of heat smacks Nulo in the face, forcing him to switch from squinting to completely closing his eyes. Nulo inhales the heavy air. "Whoa, how do they survive with this heat?"

He gallops past the soot-covered workers scooping black coals into an open damper. Nulo slows down and coughs from the suffocating heat inside his lungs. "Okay, Ribonu, I get it. This is my karma." He bends over, holding his chest and slows his pace.

A worker yells from an upper post, "Points, watch your heads down there." Nulo dives out of the way of a lowered davit and grabs the banister for balance. He rests on one knee, choking. He crawls to a nearby worker and desperately pulls at her polymer slacks for help. The boiler room supervisor turns around and sees Nulo's skin exposed to the heat. She removes her oxygen mask and places it over Nulo's face. "Here."

Nulo quickly takes several breaths of fresh air and gives her a nod of gratitude. She helps Nulo to his feet and keeps the mask on his face. The weak Nulo throws his arm over her shoulder and allows her to act as a crutch. She drags Nulo towards the nearest exhaust area and starts to get a little unsteady on her own feet.

"We're almost there," she says in a raspy voice.

They burst inside the tiny quarantine room and the heat drops tremendously. White mist is sprayed inside forcing them to wait for virus clearance. The green light pauses on yellow and Nulo's strength starts to wither. The woman shakes the knob. "Come on, come on, come on." The green light pops on and she kicks open the second door.

"Water," she yells. "I need water and coolant cards." Nearby steerage workers look up and rush over with buckets and bottled water.

Nulo, overly dehydrated, lies drenched and sucking for fresh air. His blistered skin is being soothed and treated with a specialized spray used in quarantine. Nulo's helper snatches a bottle of water for herself and looks at him incredulously.

"What are you doing down here, Nulo? You could've died and your snotty friends would've found a way to blame us for your death."

Nulo looks at all the workers and then back at her. "How do you know my name?"

"You're kidding me, right?" She points to the wall and shows hundreds of articles of Nulo hanging on the break room wall. She adds, "This whole level worships you and knows everything about you." Nulo slowly stands without uttering a word and walks over to observe the wall.

She asks, "How did you end up way down here, anyway?"

Nulo avoids the truth by taking another sip of his water. He says, "I got lost running through the combustion chamber."

"Combustion chamber? What were you doing over there?"

"Umm, I, uh." Nulo fumbles with the cap of his water bottle and accidentally drops it to the ground. He bends over to retrieve the rolling top and hears the sound of firing over his head. Nulo unintentionally dodges an AC shot. After realizing he is again being targeting, he falls to the ground for protection.

Innocent steerage workers are hit from every angle and scatter for their lives. The shots continue throughout the room and Nulo finally sees Kaphir. "You can't hide from me, super soldier. I always find my prey."

Nulo rolls behind a desk and sees his injured helper sprawled in the center of the floor. She screams in pain and reaches for the hiding Nulo. Nulo turns his AC5 on full blast and strategizes as Kaphir approaches.

Kaphir says, "That was nice work you did on my boys upstairs. I don't know how you did it all by yourself, but it was impressive. And the note you left me was clever." Kaphir aims at the desk and fires.

Nulo ducks the explosion and covers his face from the debris. He yells, "Stop! You won, okay? Let's take this elsewhere without involving these innocent workers."

"Haven't you learned that your weak speeches don't work on me?" Kaphir kicks the desk out of the way and fires.

Through the smoke, Nulo yells, "I have." Nulo punches Kaphir across the face, spins and elbows him with his opposite arm. Kaphir lands chin first and furiously fires from the ground.

Nulo dives on his back and tries to grab ahold of Kaphir's glove. Nulo slams Kaphir's skull onto the floor and is struck by Kaphir's opposing elbow. Nulo falls off and is immediately tackled against a factory furnace. Nulo grunts as his back sizzles against the scorching surface.

Kaphir scrapes his sharp elbow inside Nulo's collarbone and says, "I can play dirty if you want."

Nulo cries out in pain and desperately lifts his aiming arm.

Kaphir catches his AC and stops him. "Not so fast." Kaphir breaks Nulo's nose with a head butt. He kicks Nulo to the ground and says, "I see you got yourself some new gloves? I guess I have to break these, too."

Nulo squirms to get away, but slips in the blood that's pouring from his nose. Kaphir trails behind and just as he reaches Nulo, Kaphir is smacked across the face by the supervisor.

She kicks Kaphir over to his side and yells, "Nulo, I'll take care of him. Get out of here now." Nulo holds his neck and says, "Thanks."

"No problem." She points to a ladder suspended from the ceiling and says, "Take that chute up five floors and you'll be back on the mezzanine levels."

Nulo starts to climb, but stops. "What is your name?"

Before she answers, Kaphir fires into her back, slamming her unconscious body against a wall of lockers. Nulo yells, "Nooo!" Kaphir points his AC at Nulo and fires rapidly. Nulo dodges the shots and leaps inside the ceiling chute unharmed. He makes it to the next floor; anticipating Kaphir's fire at any moment.

"Nulo!" Kaphir yells. "We are not done yet."

Nulo grunts to pull himself up into a dark dorm hall. He jogs with a limp and checks his belt pocket for any resus cards. While holding his broken nose, he feels his burnt blisters cracking open from his rapid movement. Nulo looks over his shoulder and sees Kaphir climbing out of the hole, barking, "The hunt continues."

Nulo trips into a protruding water fountain and tumbles down on the squeaky linoleum floor. Nulo sits on his rear and points his AC5 at Kaphir as he undauntedly walks in his direction. Nulo tries to fire from his arm cannon, but only hears clicking noises and panics. "Grrr, what's wrong with this thing?" Nulo whispers.

Kaphir laughs out loud. "Still having trouble with your arm cannon?" Nulo flips over to his feet and runs while Kaphir starts firing after him.

Nulo ducks and dodges the approaching shots and dives inside a walk-in pantry. Kaphir struts through the smoking hallway. "Come out of that room so we can handle this one on one."

Kaphir hears a muffled scream from Nulo inside saying, "One on one? Why did you shoot that innocent girl down there?"

Kaphir chuckles. "Oh look at the super soldier catching feelings."

Nulo says to himself, "Ribonu, if I get out of this alive, I swear I'm going to kill you for selling me a broken AC." He looks on the side of the AC and sees a feature that reads *Safety Activated*. Nulo shakes his head and whispers, "Okay, I take back everything I said. My mistake." Nulo peeks in the hall to see how close Kaphir is, and forms a plan.

Kaphir smears the dripping blood from his head and wipes it on his shirt. He leads with his AC and shuffles towards the open pantry firing at any potential threat. Kaphir laughs maniacally and asks in the doorway, "Isn't this fun? You run for your life and I chase you? You finally met your match."

Kaphir waves the smoke away from his face, but doesn't see Nulo inside the pantry. He kicks and pushes boxes over. "Are we playing hide and seek now?" Kaphir sees a vent swinging in the back and hears footsteps sprinting up the hallway. Kaphir's eyes light up. "You slithering genius." He leans out into the hallway and splurges his ammunition at the escaping silhouette. Kaphir squares up and aims carefully at the back of the figure and shoots.

"Bull's eye," Kaphir yells while pumping his fist. He celebrates with a quick dance and asks, "When are you going to realize I'm just a better soldier than you?" Kaphir walks to the sizzling body and kicks it over. "What?"

Nulo quietly sneaks out of the pantry's door from the opposite direction of Kaphir. He discreetly returns to the tunnel ladder and yells back, "I think you missed me."

Kaphir whips around at the sound of Nulo's voice and fires without discretion. Kaphir's arm cannon flashes a red warning light indicating low ammunition. He stops and checks his count and sees the digital number '1' on the screen.

Nulo yells down the tunnel, "Uh oh, looks like you are all out of ammo, Lieutenant."

"You think I need ammo to get rid of you?" He pats his belt for more cards and realizes Nulo has picked pocketed his entire pack during the scuffle downstairs. He whispers, "I should've known." Kaphir shakes his nervousness and follows Nulo up the ladder.

. . . .

Dena laughs as she shoots a Variable scaling the wall. She looks over her shoulder and realizes Locy isn't trailing her anymore. Dena slides to a halt and scans the crossing lieutenants.

"Um, excuse me." Dena hears above her, "Are you lost or something?"

Dena looks up to see Locy at the top of the ladder, waving. Dena chuckles at her competitive friend and pouts. "Whatever." Suddenly Dena is tackled to the ground by a falling lieutenant. The apologetic soldier helps Dena back to her feet, but she unintentionally leaves behind their bag of illegal cards. Inside the bag was also the blinking cube she found earlier. Unaware of their vital loss, Dena pushes through the traffic of Variables and climbs the ladder to Locy.

Locy casually crosses her legs and yells down, "So I guess I won and you owe me points and dinner?"

Dena continues to climb the steep ladder and says, "It depends if you beat me with Variable kills or not. I have sixty."

Locy clears her throat. "Sixty-eight."

Dena rolls her eyes and scoffs. "Yeah, dinner it is."

Locy laughs out loud and forces an awkward hug by picking Dena up. While in the air, Dena catches a glimpse of Locy's TDA. "Liar!"

Locy snatches her arm behind her back. "I don't know what you are talking about."

"You know exactly what I'm talking about, cheater. You only have forty-six kills Locy."

Locy squints. "So is that a 'no' for the free meals or the points?"

"That's a no to both."

Locy pouts. "Fine, let me borrow like 500 points, so I can pay for our meals."

Dena shakes her head and playfully yanks Locy inside the mob of waiting barter escorts.

CHAPTER 13

Kaphir stomps up the ladder and instinctively stops. He taps his fingers in a wet footprint and smiles once he realizes it's Nulo's blood. Kaphir points his flashlight and follows the smeared trail leading into the shadows. "Heeey, super soldier! I just want a sincere apology for my friends you hurt downstairs. Listen, my AC is empty and I just want to talk like men." There is a long silence. Kaphir grins. "Whelp, I see you still want to take the other route."

"I do!" A thunderous blast illuminates the hall and strikes Kaphir in the stomach. He slides on his back a few feet and rolls completely over onto his face. Nulo appears as a silhouette through a cloud of dust with his smoking AC5 by his side.

Kaphir holds his chest and asks, "Wait, I thought your glove was deactivated?"

Nulo backhands Kaphir across the face and says, "It was."

Kaphir sees the shiny glazed upgraded model and begins to scoot backward. "Come on, Nulo, you know this isn't fair. I'm empty. I was just playing earlier. I wasn't really going to kill you."

Nulo ignores the pleading and follows Kaphir as he slides helplessly on his elbows. Nulo laughs. "Doesn't this look so familiar? Wow how the tables have turned."

"Listen. Everything I said and did was an act for my crew. I was just having some fun before I got promoted."

"Fun, that's what you call it?" Nulo increases the voltage on his AC5 and fires an explosion between Kaphir's legs.

The ground crumbles into a massive hole and Kaphir's voice cracks, "Whoa. Okay, okay, I'm sorry."

"Sorry? You thought it'd be that easy? You thought I would say, *oh no worries*, we'd shake hands and be best friends from now on? No!" Nulo punts Kaphir in his stomach. "You have no idea what I've been through because of you." Nulo charges forward, punching him repeatedly in his patched eye until the strap rips off Kaphir's face.

Kaphir's head bounces in Nulo's grip and collapses onto the ground. He turns back, weakened with a deep gash joining his already stitched eye. Kaphir squints through his good eye and tries to plug the blood out its vision. He feels around and contemplates when to use his remaining shot. Kaphir looks over his shoulder and sees a surveillance camera under a spotlight and baits Nulo to follow him. "Please. Think about what you are doing. You don't want to kill an innocent soldier do you?"

Nulo catches the slick insult. "You got a lot of nerve if you think mocking me in your position is the best idea." Emotionally, Nulo raises his voice, "I practically died in the bistro. You took my TDA so I couldn't heal. I don't believe you were *just playing*. I should take your glove off and swing a few rounds across your face. How would you like that?"

Kaphir gets in position of the camera and says, "No, Nulo, this isn't you at all."

"Isn't me?" Nulo suddenly pitches an underhanded fireball at his foe, but Kaphir flips back to his stomach and avoids the shot. Nulo ignites another haywire shot at him, but again misses. Kaphir backs himself onto a crumbling peninsula in the floor and realizes Nulo's stray shots were on purpose.

170

Approaching with a devilish grin, Nulo states, "In the words of Kaphir, how does it feel to be inefficient; punished and powerless just like that? It hurts doesn't it?"

"Alright, we're even. I'm sorry."

"Naw, he hasn't had enough until I say so. Remember that?"

Kaphir cries out, "But I didn't go this far. You know I could've killed you, but I didn't."

"But you did kill me. You removed everything I had because of your pettiness."

"Petty? Look at what you are doing. I said I was sorry. What else do you want from me?"

"I want you to remember my face whenever you feel like you're untouchable."

Nulo slowly walks around the broken pieces of the wall and points his AC5. "Nulo, Lieutenant Nulo, please come in, over."

Nulo looks down at his TDA and hears Ghii. "Nulo, respond now. Please report to the inquiry level immediately."

As Nulo listens to Ghii's request, Kaphir says, relieved, "You see, I'm always a step ahead of you. Now the entire ship will see their deranged idol in action." Kaphir points to the aiming camera behind Nulo. While Nulo looks to find the camera, Kaphir fires his last shot at Nulo's head.

The sudden sound forces Nulo to flinch out of the way and allows the shot to destroy the camera. Simultaneously the recoil from Kaphir's AC catapults him through the slippery debris and tosses him off the broken peninsula. Nulo runs to Kaphir's aid, but he's gone. Kaphir yells for his life and falls three levels down into a high traffic courtyard.

Kaphir smacks the ground with an audible splat, lifeless. Nearby witnesses are startled by the falling body and look up to see Nulo's head and arm hanging out of the hole. Nulo quickly pulls himself back, which makes him look guilty.

"He's dead," Nulo hears as he crawls away. He holds his head in total shock and knows the amount of trouble he is in. Nulo jumps up and takes off running.

. . . .

Dena and Locy finally approach the front of the barter lines. Dena looks past the numerous escorts, hoping to spot Riti waiting as well. She picks up the required MEG crate and moves forward. Locy, a few escorts behind Dena, follows suit.

Reality finally sets in with Dena. She looks back at the Arvelee and feels as if everything is moving in slow motion. The clustering sound around Dena abruptly mutes and she can literally hear her heart beating with her footsteps. She swallows the gravity of her decision with hopes of getting closer to the answers she seeks.

Dena reaches to insert her boarding card and discovers her bag is missing. She quickly switches the box to her other hand and franticly examines her clothing.

Dena panics. She turns towards Locy and secretly signals her for help. Locy frowns and Dena pops her eyes open even wider to insinuate trouble. The Arvelee escort behind Dena nudges her forward. "Keep moving." Dena obediently approaches the Tamin barter officer, but doesn't raise her wrist under the scanner.

The chunky Tamin officer eagerly gestures for Dena to scan her TDA, but she doesn't budge. He yells in his home language, which makes Dena panic even more. Locy finally pops up to create a distraction. "Is everything okay?" Dena scoots behind Locy and pushes her towards the officer. Locy explains, "I'm sorry is her first barter and I'm training her." Unaware of what she just said, the officer snatches Locy's wrist to scan her TDA instead.

Dena gasps as the scanners reads "Clear."

The Tamin officer shoves Locy out the way and reaches for Dena to be next. Locy turns to see Dena accidentally fumbles her case and drops it on the officer's foot. The case cracks open and the tiny MEG capsules scatter in different directions. "I'm sorry, sorry," Dena cries.

The chunky officer falls and reaches down to his throbbing toe in agony. Another Tamin officer pushes Dena out of the way and yells with an accent, "Get out of here."

Dena quickly picks up what she can from the shattered pieces and scurries onto the Tamin.

Locy pulls Dena inside an emergency door and up a stairwell. She rips off an arena vent and crawls inside. "Come on, Dena, hurry."

Dena follows as they crawl quickly through the mezzanine walls of the Tamin. Locy and Dena make a few turns and reach a closed vent on the wall. Locy tilts the shutters open and peeks through. She kicks the vent off the hinges and crawls through the panel. Dena follows Locy into the Tamin's hall, overwhelmed with disbelief.

Locy announces, "Okay, when your heart stops racing I want you to know we've done it."

Dena hugs Locy, eyes full of tears, and cries, "We made it?"

"Yes," Locy confirms. "But what happened back there? Why did you freeze up?"

"I must've dropped our bag of cards somewhere. He would've busted me as soon as I scanned my TDA."

"I knew it was something as soon as you gave me that weird look. Don't worry, I'm sure we can find another Cove or card dealer on board. We just got to stay in the dark and keep a low profile."

"Agreed!" Dena grabs Locy's wrist. "How did you get your glove to clear?"

Locy chuckles. "I pickpocketed that dorky officer in between us."

"You stole that poor guy's boarding card?"

"It's the temporary one, but yeah." Locy laughs and asks, "But what about you? You're the one who dropped that fifteen pound box onto that officer's foot."

Dena realizes she helped the escape and says, "You're not the only one with a few tricks up their sleeve."

"Well, it was perfect timing because I was all out of ideas for you." The two hug once more and prepare for their new journey.

. . . .

Arooni knocks on the captain's chamber door and is overcome with nervousness. "Captain Lyme? It's Director Arooni."

"Come in, Director."

Arooni pushes the door forward and exhales deeply. She sees Captain Lyme meditating on her knees with lit candles all around. Arooni loosely attempts to explain her predicament to the prophetic captain. She softly says, "I'm sorry to disturb your stimulation again, but we're in search of a phage's location. He must've removed his TDA beacon because we can't find him on the ship's GPS."

Captain Lyme keeps her back towards Arooni, wipes the tears from her face and asks, "Is it Nulo?"

"Yes ma'am. Can you locate him through your Aberash?" Captain Lyme finally turns around. "I'll do what I can."

Suddenly Paxo yells from the hallway. "Captain Lyme, Arooni are you in there?"

"Yes."

He slides the steel door open and rushes in. "We just received word that Lieutenant Nulo has murdered another soldier." Captain Lyme remains calm, closes her eyes and continues her meditation.

Arooni turns to Captain Lyme and asks, "You knew all of this was going to happen, didn't you?"

"Yes. We can't escape events due to come."

"So what should I do now?"

Captain Lyme beckons for Arooni to come near. "Pray with me. You and the leadership of the Arvelee will need it."

Paxo clears his throat to get Arooni's attention and he mouths, "We don't have enough time."

Arooni nods. "I'm gonna have to take a rain check on that. But as soon as the ship is in better shape, I promise to come back and pray with you."

Saddened, Captain Lyme exhales. "Okay."

As Arooni turns to exit, Captain Lyme says, "Be patient with your soldier's director and watch what you say. Have a swift ear to listen and a slow tongue in speech."

"Okay?" Arooni awkwardly exits with Paxo to the hallway. "That was odd. The Captain obviously sees something she can't tell us and that worries me."

"Yeah, she always freaks me out. But follow me, you have to see this."

Arooni jogs behind Paxo back to the receptionist area. Paxo flops in the swivel chair and rewinds the surveillance. "This is some of the footage we found of Nulo, right before the cameras went out. We first found him in the balcony's bistro and later saw him entering the promenade. He disappeared for a while, but a steerage worker said they saw him down in the boiler room."

Arooni zooms in on Nulo's face. "So what do we know about him?"

"Other than his incredible fighting skills and arrogant attitude, he's clean. There are no motives or history between the two lieutenants, but there are a lot of eye witnesses that say Nulo did it."

"Contact the barter officers and abort this Tamin barter immediately. Nulo knows there isn't anywhere to hide on this ship. My guess, he's now planning an escape."

"I'll make the call."

"Prepare for a full lockdown."

Paxo quickly announces throughout the ship, "Calling all active maphletes, be on the lookout for the armed and dangerous, Lieutenant Nulo; last seen on the ballroom level. Suspect is armed with an unregistered AC. Bring him to the inquiry suites alive."

Dr. Ribonu overhears the announcement in disgust and drops his head inside his hands. He sits across from Sharlo, inside her empty diner, and wipes a tear from her cheek. Ribonu kisses the medallion around his neck and locks hands with Sharlo. "We did all we could. All we can do now is pray."

Sharlo closes her eyes and tries to concentrate, but cries out, "Is this really happening now? I was told the war wouldn't take place for another hundred years."

"Only the Aberash knows the hour of the event. We can only hope that we find Nulo in time."

. . . .

Opha, Ghii and Esko silently wait in inquiry suite 2A. Esko stands with a huge grin on his face, basking in his well-orchestrated plan. He quietly leans over to Ghii. "You see? I told you everything happens for a reason."

Opha blurts, "You guys are pathetic."

"We're pathetic?" Esko asks. "We're not fugitives wanted for murder like your friend." Opha folds his arms and mumbles, "Whatever."

Esko laughs. "Soon our names will be cleared and Arooni will see that this whole thing was just good leadership."

. . . .

All around the ship, maphletes activate their heel rockets and fly high and low searching for Nulo. The barter officers are instructed that they are on mandatory lockdown and are restricted from crossing the planks. Both ship's officers panic and evacuate the scheduled transactions. Every active TDA displays a flashing wanted picture of Lieutenant Nulo and a list of his committed crimes. Citizens are shocked and their loyalty to Nulo is broken; their once admired hero is now a murderer.

An hour passes and not one sighting of Lieutenant Nulo has been reported. Due to an imposed curfew, the ship's halls are clear. The flickering backup lights struggle to illuminate hallways.

A couple of maphletes come across a few of the same blinking cubes that have been spotted throughout the ship and analyze them amongst themselves. "What are these things?"

"I don't know, but we should take them up and see if Paxo can figure it out."

The entire mezzanine level blacks out, lit only by the maphletes' arm cannon lights and heel rockets, causing a roaring reaction from the patrolling officers. "We've lost power on the mezzanine," screams a concerned maphlete over her TDA. Two maphletes land on the surface, extinguishing their only source of light.

"We are literally flying blind. Can someone help us down here with some lights?"

No response except static. The two maphletes settle and scoot forward with the assistance of the glow from their TDA.

.   .   .   .

Maphlete Paxo discreetly drags Arooni inside the presidential gauge room, also known as the PGR. Paxo closes the door behind Arooni and quietly reveals his concern. "I think it's time for the ship to regroup and come up with a safer strategy."

"What's the problem now?"

"I'm not certain, but we really need to be on guard for whatever is about to come. I've studied this ship front to back and never have I seen a chain of reactions like this." Paxo pulls out a tablet blueprint of the Arvelee and points out irregular knots.

Paxo continues, "As you know, when Nicil is dropped, we essentially become exposed to anything by default, the ship disperses a vaccine for us and quarantines the point of attack. Well, when I opened the backup vents, it temporarily inhaled the Nicil mist, but the EMP malfunctioned the filtering of the toxins. Once the backup generators go out, it will exhale the Nicil mist back into the arenas."

"What? That's insane."

"I agree and that's why I said I think we're under attack."

"How could this happen?"

"Worst case scenario, someone on board is trying to kill us."

"I guess this is what the captain was trying to tell me."

"Probably. It's definitely someone who knows the Arvelee inside and out." Paxo's tablet vibrates and he switches screens to see more daunting news. "Oh no, look. A fleet of Variables are crawling inside the rear foyer. The plank door appears jammed and the arena is unguarded due to the curfew."

Arooni watches the infestation from the tablet. "They can't get inside the main ship, right?"

"Luckily they're locked inside the arena. The Nicil mist will soon reverse and kill them all." "But not enough to keep them out until we fully recover."

Arooni flips over a couch and turns back to Paxo. "What about gas masks?"

Paxo adjusts his goggles. "The new Nicil powder is strong and will rip through our skin and oxygen tanks."

Arooni snatches the tablet and flips through for more options. "Where are the two commanders that were supposed to be in there in the first place?"

Paxo checks the ship's schedule. "That would be Commanders Locy and Dena. I'm seeing that they never scanned in for their shifts. That's strange. They're both registered for Variable kills on the mezzanine this past shift. This must be some sort of mistake."

"Or exactly what they want us to think. They are your suspects, Paxo. Find them now. Like you said, all this didn't happen by coincidence. It was orchestrated from the inside."

. . . .

Captain Lyme does her part and prepares to search for Lieutenant Nulo. She grabs her temples and channels her alpha spirit to connect to Nulo's mind. The lit candles dance in unison and twirl with her every emotion. The Captain reaches a spiritual pinnacle and begins to levitate in mid-air. Captain Lyme's eyes turn ivory, her dress begins to flow as the room is filled with a sudden gust of wind and her body is tossed back and forth. She drops to a runner's position and whispers, "There you are." She envisions Nulo running at full speed in stolen clothing through a crowd of pedestrians. He inconspicuously weaves through foot traffic toward an unknown destination. She disconnects from the sighting and weeps into her hands.

The captain gathers herself and discreetly enters a tiny hole tucked away and crawls through a tunnel. She reaches the admiral's bridge and carefully pushes the door open. While still on all fours, she whispers in many tongues to summon the admiral. Captain Lyme shivers with chills, causing her eyelids to flicker open. Her muscles deflate once she feels the presences of the mighty Admiral Arvelee approaching.

His deep, aggrandized voice vibrates her chest. "Speak!"

Lyme keeps her forehead pressed to the ground and begs, "Admiral, may I open my eyes to speak with you? What I predicted has commenced and the war has started." Admiral Arvelee stares at the worshipping captain and reveals himself without responding. He reaches down to grab Captain Lyme's hand and helps her up to her feet. She pans up to see an enormous, twenty foot high Admiral Arvelee glowing before her.

His amplified breathing echoes off the walls. He asks, "Has everyone on board discovered the Aberash?"

"No, not yet, but a few of them are really close."

"Only a few? This is not what the prophecy predicted. You do know our world is in grave danger. Someone has changed the course of our future and we might not be prepared."

"I understand, my lord, but I trust our selected team soldiers." The admiral walks away from her and hangs his head. He adjusts his draping robe and Captain Lyme reassures him by saying, "I beg of you to trust the Aberash with me. Despite our soldier's ignorance, we know all things work for the greater good for their purpose. Many lives will be lost in this war and now we'll need your ability to birth a newer generation of phages more than ever."

Admiral Arvelee grants her request with a pessimistic nod.

About the Author

Hailing from Dayton Ohio, Dion Lack is a writer making major waves in the entertainment industry. After years of working as a sketch and screenwriter, Dion has added author to his resume. "The Voyage of Truth" is the debut novel that introduces the readers to Dion's vivid imagination in science fiction. This forever evolving Renaissance man now resides in Los Angeles with his wife and children.

VOYAGE OF TRUTH

Character Sketch Book
Illustrations by Nizar Ilman

DENA

Senior commander of the
Arvelee. A leading woman
with unshakable morals.
Dena is a phenomenal
sniper with surprising
hand to hand combat.
Inspired by her best friend
Locy, Dena begins to
question everything.

NULO

Nulo is the most talked
about soldier on board for
good and bad reasons.
He's arrogant and
purposefully gets under
everyone's skins. Nulo
strives to be the greatest
solider on the planet.

GRAE

Notorious for being the rebel of the Arvelee. Grae enjoys staying under the radar. Quick talking, card dealer that despises ship ordinance, Grae stays in trouble. He is driven by power and wealth. He once had a relationship with Nushaka, which he hasn't fully gotten over.

LOCY

The brazen, fast talking commander of the Arvelee, Locy is an egalitarian obsessed with conspiracies. Best friends with Dena, she is experiencing a spiritual breakthrough.

ESKO

A brilliant maphlete, native of the Arvelee. Suffers from bitterness but obsessed with power. A respected soldiers known for his iconic tactics. Formerly a part of an inseparable trio (Nulo & Ghii) but crumbles over a life changing accident.

KAPHIR

A wicked lieutenant with a large chip on his shoulder. Kaphir is a bully with a weak mind and an inability to let go of a grudge. He lets his small quarrel with Nulo fester into fatal blows.

NUSHAKA

A bold, Arvelee lieutenant with a brilliant mind. Nushaka is an innovator who can possibly change the world. After moving on from Grae, she finally decides to come forth to her longtime admirer.

OPHA

Best described as old fashioned, Opha is one of the few lieutenants that carry melee weapons on the Arvelee. Pegged as the gentle giant, he is the only one Nulo claims as a friend.

AROONI

The director of the Arvelee. She is the most powerful woman on the board and runs a tight ship. She's the youngest to be appointed this position and the other candidates despise her for it. She is paranoid of the idea an uprising.

LYME

The loving captain of the Arvelee. Lyme is omniscient and omnipotent. She reveals her powers only to align purpose. Her identity remains a mysterious.

RIBONU

The black market physician who provides select soldiers wisdom and truth. Ribonu lives under the radar with Sharlo. He's one of the few on board that believes in restoration especially in Nulo.

SHARLO

The owner of the self-titled bistro of the Arvelee. She's an ear to many troubled lieutenants and works closely with Ribonu. She's witty and very trust worthy.

FRAYZA

A money driven lieutenant of the Mershon. He's short tempered and lacks strong morals. Frayza's life partner is Coya.

X

A walking virus that exclusively attacks citizens on any and every ship. No mentioned motives behind his sudden killing rampage.

Paxo

The brains of the Arvelee. Paxo is extremely strategic and optimizes the issues with precession. He is the problem solver for Arooni and loves the challenge of his position. Paxo is Arooni's apprentice and right hand man.

Riti

The pirate of division 5. He's an unknown outsider that jumps from ship to ship. His origin has never been determined due to his ever-changing stories. Riti, full of wisdom with big plans of his own.

ORASHI

A radical lieutenant of the Mershon. She's mysterious with a disclosed, battered past. Orashi's mouth has gotten her into a lot of trouble but that doesn't stop her annoying curiosity.

GHII

Ghii is the braun of the Arvelee and is close friends with Esko. He's big on unity and loves his home.

KULINDA

The appointed leader of the Iotas. She's abrasive and extremely intimidating. Kulinda is full of secrets and enjoys the weight she holds on her shoulders.

SULTRI

One of the overlooked lieutenants on the Arvelee. He is incredible at what he does but will always be in Nulo's shadows. He strives for equality but is repeatedly ignored by maphletes.

FOTORIA

The Arvelee's secretary on the presidential level. She's timid, easily influenced and hates controversy. Fotaria and Sultri are dating.

www.ingramcontent.com/pod-product-compliance
Lightning Source LLC
Chambersburg PA
CBHW020409150626
46554CB00012B/426